"That was unforgivable, not to mention horribly ungallant."

Verity felt the warmth stealing into her cheeks but resolutely ignored it. "And the next time it happens? Will you be able to refrain from being horribly ungallant again? And again?" she said gently.

Brad looked at her thoughtfully, then raised an eyebrow. "If you don't kiss me back the next time, I might."

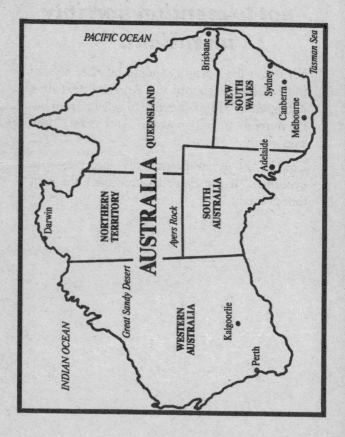

LINDSAY ARMSTRONG

A Dangerous Lover

Harlequin Books

TORONTO • NEW YORK • LONDON
AMSTERDAM • PARIS • SYDNEY • HAMBURG
STOCKHOLM • ATHENS • TOKYO • MILAN
MADRID • WARSAW • BUDAPEST • AUCKLAND

Harlequin Presents first edition April 1993
ISBN 0-373-11546-6

Original hardcover edition published in 1992
by Mills & Boon Limited

A DANGEROUS LOVER

CHAPTER ONE

'I NEED a pair of twins. Preferably redheads with freckles, and I'd like the boy to have a particularly mischievous look and—no, let's make it the other way round. The girl should be a real tomboy and the boy a bookish type—what's so difficult about that?'

Verity Wood grimaced as she strode down the corridor, for her boss's voice was clearly audible and his mood all too familiar; and she guessed he would be surrounded by several anxious, nervous people who had not the slightest idea of how to deal with Brad Morris on these occasions.

She was almost right, she discovered as she entered the office. There was the girl from the typing pool whom she'd asked to deputise for her this morning and who was close to tears. There was Tim Cameron, office manager, looking very stern, and William Morris, Brad's brother and head of the Morris Advertising Agency, wearing a dark suit and waistcoat and the lugubrious expression he so often wore when confronted by his brilliant but erratic sibling. And finally there was Primrose Carpenter, the only one looking faintly amused, but stunningly beautiful as always.

No one noticed Verity enter as Brad Morris continued in a mixture of tones that was both sardonic and scathing with a dash of plaintiveness thrown in for good measure. 'I mean to say, you are asking me not only to advertise this very ordinary little household item, but also to persuade sixteen million Australians to dash out and purchase one, yet you treat my simplest request as if I'm asking to go to the moon. Indeed, it would probably be easier *to* go to the moon...'

Verity raised her unusually golden hazel eyes heavenwards and stepped forward. 'There is no problem, Mr Morris,' she said evenly, and restrained herself from adding 'apart from yourself'.

Everyone swung round, although in Brad Morris's case this merely involved swivelling the chair he was reclining in a couple of notches. He did not remove his long legs from the desk, nor did he remove his hands from behind his head. And he said nothing for a long moment but he used that moment to full effect as he scanned Verity from top to toe, from her cropped golden-red hair, *her* freckles, her white fitted jacket, her short black skirt and her long legs encased in sheer black stockings to her elegant court shoes with little heels and back to her hands with their short nails and no nail polish. Then he drawled, 'I do believe Mrs Wood has deigned to grace us with her presence. How fortunate we are!'

During the two years she'd worked for him Verity had longed to hit Brad Morris on occasions, and this was another of them, she discovered, and was not helped by the fact that she'd spent a difficult morning, but she breathed deeply and sought for the cool formality with which she normally treated him. 'I was not aware you were coming in this morning, Mr Morris, otherwise I would have been here,' she said equably and then found she didn't feel particularly equable. 'In fact,' she continued, 'in lieu of any information to the contrary, I assumed you were still holidaying in the Whitsundays. However, if after six weeks of procrastination you've finally decided to get to work on the Pearson account, may I say that, considering how much time I've spent fobbing Mr Pearson off, not to mention actually lying to him, it's not *before* time?'

The silence was electric. The girl from the typing pool seemed incapable of closing her mouth and even Primrose looked startled.

As for Brad Morris, he unwound his tall, wiry frame from chair and desk and stood up leisurely. As always, he scorned his brother's more conventional attire and wore khaki trousers with a check shirt and suede boots. His brown curly hair looked as wild as it usually did and his rather Roman nose prominent. Yet there was something amazingly attractive about him to women, Verity had discovered. She'd put it down at first to his tall, thin gangliness arousing their maternal instincts, but had had that apparently disproved to her often enough to strenuously doubt it now. But he doesn't attract me, she reminded herself, and she waited for him to retaliate as she knew he would. Then she thought—why wait?

'After all,' she said casually but with a cutting little edge, 'we all *know* you're a genius of a kind. We all know you have a remarkable talent for handling children and animals and their owners and their parents and that you make wonderful ads, but they *are* only ads, here today, forgotten tomorrow, and it really doesn't, one would have thought, entitle you to act like a cross between Shakespeare and Van Gogh. It can't be that weighty a muse, surely?'

There was no electric silence this time. Tim Cameron moved restlessly, the typist shut her mouth with an audible click of her teeth and William Morris cleared his throat preparatory to speaking, but his brother beat him to it.

'Don't bother to defend me, Billy,' he said sweetly, causing William to look momentarily pained. 'Unfortunately, since *Mr* Wood's—er—untimely demise, whoever has been sleeping with Mrs Wood hasn't been doing a great job of it. Either that or no one has. But,' he gestured genially, 'I'm quite used to dealing with these frustrated, spinsterish outbursts. Primrose, darling,' he turned to her, 'I was going to take you out to lunch, but as you can see things are a little out of control here, so would you mind getting yourself a cab home?'

Primrose Carpenter withdrew her lovely violet gaze from Verity with an effort and said with a tinge of exasperation, 'Brad, we were on the way home from the airport in *my* car when you became infused with inspiration and insisted on coming here!'

'That's true,' he replied gravely. 'I'd forgotten. But that even simplifies things. If you could retrieve my bag from your boot and give it to—Tim?'

'Brad—yes, of course,' Primrose said but with a tinge of confusion and something else darkening her eyes.

'I'm sorry things have happened this way, Primmy,' Brad Morris said and stopped rather abruptly, with the lines and angles of his face set into an expression that was curiously withdrawn for a moment. Then it was as if he made a conscious effort to break that moment, and he said lightly, although there was no mistaking the look of deep affection and tenderness in his grey eyes as they rested on her, 'But chin up, darling! I'll give you a buzz tonight.' He turned to Tim Cameron. 'Tim?'

'Yes, fine,' Tim Cameron said hastily. 'I'll come and get it, Primrose. Er...' But he didn't have to say any more; perhaps Verity's expression said it all, because everyone then trooped out with alacrity, excepting perhaps Primrose, who cast Brad one last, lingering glance.

Brad Morris waited until the door was closed, then he leant his fists on the desk and said, 'Before you hit me, Mrs Wood, why don't you tell me what's biting you?'

'*You* are what's biting me, Mr Morris——'

'I can assure you, Mrs Wood,' he drawled, 'I am not. I don't go around biting women unless I'm invited to, and then I do it in the nicest possible way.'

Verity ground her teeth in frustration.

He went on when she found it impossible to speak, 'Is that really the problem? I mean, the lack of some man to bite you nicely? If so, why is it such a problem? By my reckoning, you've been a widow for over two years now and no one would expect you to remain faithful to a memory forever. Particularly if it's interfering with your state of mind——'

'Mr M-Morris,' Verity still had difficulty articulating, so angry was she now, 'I must warn you not to continue in this vein, because I'm liable to do more than hit you, believe me.'

He looked her up and down with a satirically raised eyebrow. 'All right, have a go,' he invited. 'It might just relieve some of the pressure. Are you a black-belt karate expert in disguise, though? Because if you are I don't think that would be quite fair. I'm not, you see. And, on second thoughts, I might object to being tossed over your shoulder and thrown heavily to the floor. What I had more in mind was for you to pound your fists uselessly against my manly chest—something along those lines.' He grimaced. 'I—er—might have miscalculated.' His gaze roamed down her body again. 'To the extent that you're not exactly a fragile little flower of a girl—how could I have forgotten?' he marvelled. 'But our very own trim, fit, athletic Mrs Wood—much more a fitting Jane-for-Tarzan-type, really. I will retract that offer, Mrs Wood,' he said gravely. 'But, should you like to pound the desk instead—be my guest.'

Verity stared at him for a full minute, during which she fought a pitched battle with her emotions and was further incensed to see him watching the way her breasts heaved beneath the white linen; then she swung away and strode to her desk. 'That's the last time you'll insult me, Mr Morris,' she said precisely, and sat down and started opening drawers and relieving them of their contents with fiercely controlled movements.

He looked slightly amused and strolled over to lean against the wall next to the desk. 'Which bit?' he queried after a moment.

'*What* bit?'

'Was so insulting?'

'All of it!'

'Ah. Then you don't see yourself as having the kind of figure Tarzan would have enjoyed? Perhaps I was a bit unkind there. To tell the truth, Mrs Wood, you have a wonderful slim, lissom figure, with incredible legs, and I should imagine few men alive could resist it.'

The phone rang before Verity could reply, and in fact she picked it up only because she was afraid of what else she might do. 'Hello!'

'Mrs Wood? It's Len Pearson here!'

She took a breath and lay back in her chair. '*Hello*, Mr Pearson,' she said brightly. 'How are you today? I'm sure you're ringing to find out if I've been able to pin Mr Morris down and actually get him to start work on your account,' she went on without waiting for a reply. 'Unfortunately I have some bad news for you. He is here—oh, by the way, he was never as busy as I've led you to believe these past weeks, I was simply covering for him while he lazed in the sun in the Whitsundays. But the bad news is, although he *is* here now, I've decided to—er—part company with him. Now that might not seem an earth-shattering event to you, Mr Pearson, but, believe me, it's going to be an absolute disaster. Mr Morris is incredibly difficult to work for, and without me to do the ground work for him in this advertising campaign he will be simply lost. Incidentally, to make matters worse, he actually views your *wonderful* invention as "a very ordinary little household item", quote, unquote, so—well, be that as it may, it will also take him ages to find someone to replace me. Not that there aren't plenty of people out there who could do the job, but people who could actually tolerate working for Mr Morris would have to be as rare as hens' teeth. So I would suggest, Mr Pearson,' she said sweetly, 'that you give serious consideration to taking your account elsewhere. Goodbye. Do have a nice day.'

She put the phone down and looked up at Brad Morris defiantly, to see that he was laughing silently.

Then he said softly, 'Bravo, Mrs Wood. In this game of tit for tat, that was a stroke of genius. I salute you!'

Verity closed her eyes then stood up, heaved the shopping bag she'd brought to work on to the desk, shovelled her belongings into it and looked around for her bag.

He straightened at last. 'Oh, come now. Can't we call it quits? Believe me, you've routed me utterly. Can you just imagine the lengths I'm going to have to go to soothe Pearson's wounded vanity? He seriously believes he's come up with the eighth wonder of the world.'

'If I thought for one moment you *yourself* would go to any lengths——' She broke off with a disgusted sound. 'No, I'm going anyway, I've had enough——'

He moved closer—so that he was standing right beside her, in fact. At six feet two to her five feet eight, he was nearly a head taller than she was, but she raised her eyes to his and there was a clear warning in them; also a lot of anger.

But he studied her unworriedly and with a glint in his grey eyes she recognised only too well—the advance notice that he was about to do something outrageous. She stiffened and started to say something, but he put his hand on her wrist and overrode her, 'There is another way we could resolve this, Verity.'

She stilled. 'Don't call me that.'

'Why not? How ridiculous is it to work with someone for two years and insist on being called "Mrs Wood" all the time as if you were at least sixty and a genuine spinster into the bargain? To my mind it's all part of the problem, and it's about time I did something about it. So you may call me Mr Morris until the cows come home but I shall call you Verity from now on—and I'll also do this.' He paused and smiled faintly. 'Do note that I have you boxed into a corner, Verity, in the cowardly interests of my wind and limb, I must admit, but also in *your* best interests.'

And, as she only had time to take a startled breath, he pulled her into his arms.

'No...' she whispered incredulously, stunned into immobility.

'Yes,' he murmured. 'In fact, quite definitely so. How does it feel?' His grey gaze rested on her parted lips, the colour flooding into her cheeks. 'I have to say that for me it feels rather good, but it would be even better if you could relax.'

Verity made a convulsive movement and at the same time made a discovery that surprised her: Brad Morris might be tall and wiry but he was also stronger than she was, a lot stronger—so much so that without exerting much effort at all and without hurting her he was quite capable of holding her in his arms against her will.

'Let me go,' she said shakily.

He shook his head, his eyes amused. 'Not until I've done what I set out to do.' He moved his hands and gathered her closer so that her body was resting against his. 'An amazing handful, Mrs Wood.' His lips twisted. 'That just slipped out, sorry. The Mrs Wood bit. The rest is all too true. *Do* you sleep with anyone these days?'

Verity stared up into his eyes and knew from the suddenly heavy-lidded way he was looking at her that, however this had started out and whether or not Brad

Morris had intended merely to tease her, he now fully intended to kiss her.

She gathered all her resources and warned herself to stay calm. 'No. I don't intend to, either, so you may as well let me go, Mr Morris. If nothing else, wouldn't you say it's a little undignified what you're doing?'

He laughed quietly and slid one hand up the back of her neck and into her hair. 'I never rested on my dignity, Verity. You of all people should know that.' And he bent his head and started to do just what she'd feared.

She did struggle then, and despite the uselessness of it—at least the uselessness of trying to free herself—she managed to evade his mouth quite successfully. But he merely lifted his head until she stopped struggling and said gravely, 'Not a good way to begin, apparently. Tell me how you like to start. I shall bow to your preferences.'

Verity was breathing heavily. 'My current preference,' she said raggedly, 'would be to see you struck down by a bolt of lightning before my eyes!'

He grinned, then his eyes sobered. 'I'm going to do it, you know. You could always close your eyes and think of England, not that I would dream of going that far, but all the same...' He shrugged and loosened his arms slightly and simply waited. But his eyes never left hers.

Verity swallowed, then heard herself saying huskily, '*Why*?' And immediately coloured again and bit her lip.

'Why?' He considered and allowed his long fingers to roam through her hair again. 'There is this spontaneous sort of combustion flowing between us today,

Verity,' he said musingly. 'You took one look at me and were obviously possessed of an uprush of emotion that made you want to, if not kill me, squash me as flat as you could. And almost simultaneously I was moved to retaliate as humiliatingly as I could. Since we have no real reason to hate each other, it occurred to me that the cause of all this,' he smiled slightly, 'overheatedness might be something else altogether. It generally is between persons of the opposite sex. Have you ever worn your hair long?'

'Yes. And no,' Verity said. 'I——'

'Why did you cut it? It's a wonderful colour and I like the texture.'

Verity closed her eyes frustratedly and then flinched as he drew his fingers down her cheek.

If he noticed he made no comment. 'As for your freckles,' he went on, 'they're like a gold-dusting on your skin. I know this is a very obvious question, but are they all over you?' His hand left her skin, but only briefly, to slide under her jacket. 'You were saying?'

She opened her eyes and stared into his. 'Don't you ever give up, Mr Morris?'

He grimaced. 'Not often. But tell me. You said yes. And no.'

'Yes, I have worn my hair long, and no, I don't believe this "overheatedness" has to do with anything other than the fact that you are impossible sometimes. You must *know* you are.'

'Sometimes,' he agreed, and then as her eyes glinted an ironic gold he said wryly, 'All right, often. But normally *you* never have any trouble coping with me. Why not today?'

Verity sighed unwittingly and then, because he had a point, and because she didn't seem to be getting anywhere by any other means, said, 'I had some awkward business to settle this morning. It left me in a—very tense mood.'

'What was it?'

'Nothing.' She bit her lip at his sardonic look. 'It was private.'

'I wouldn't shout it from the roof-tops.'

'Nevertheless, it is *my* business, Mr Morris. If,' she continued with an effort, 'I allowed it to...colour my dealings with you this morning I apologise, but you were also going out of your way to be provocative.'

'Provocative,' he mused, and Verity suddenly realised that he was now trailing his fingers up and down her spine, lightly, beneath her jacket, and almost absently, and it was—she swallowed—oddly reassuring.

His lips twisted. 'Then, I, too, apologise,' he said, 'with a flourish! I mean,' he explained, 'there is surely no better way for two people to make up after an argument than this!' And he bent his head and kissed her lightly on the lips.

Verity neither protested nor responded, but she did feel herself relaxing a little—and that proved fatal. A trap, she had to acknowledge, as much for herself as it might have been for him. But as her taut body softened slightly it was as if the full impact of being in his arms hit her. It was as if her senses were being bombarded with the sheer potent attraction of Brad Morris that she'd tried for so long to deny or to decry.

It was as if they were suddenly caught in an electro-magnetic field that caused all else to fade by comparison, the office, the building, the noises outside the door, everything but this amazing awareness of each other. In fact, all Verity could think was how right his hard lines felt against her, how the feel of his arms around her and his hands on her back and hips were causing her body, which had been so chaste for so long, to flower within and without and to tremble with anticipation. How she seemed to be drowning in his clever, intent gaze and how her mouth suddenly felt luscious and kissable, her breasts achingly sensitive—and how not to be kissed and caressed would leave her feeling like an empty void.

And, as it all hit her, her lips parted, and she flushed hectically this time, and he said something inaudible and claimed her mouth.

It was a deep, searching kiss, and when she finally broke away he let her, but moved his hands more and more intimately on her, flicking the buttons of her jacket open and cradling her body to his.

'No...' It was more a breath of sound than anything as the feeling of his fingers on her skin, slipping beneath her bra, brought her back to some sanity.

'Yes,' he murmured and started to kiss her again, and somehow, she wasn't sure how, their positions changed so that she had her arms around his neck and he was free to find the front clasp of her bra and to release it and span her waist beneath the swell of her breasts, then move his hands slowly upwards until he could touch her nipples with his thumbs and inflict a kind of gasping delight on her that ran right through her body.

What would have happened next was something Verity refused to allow herself to dwell on, but at that moment someone knocked on the door.

She froze, and her eyes flew open as Brad lifted his head and she found herself looking into his eyes and seeing the wry expression in them.

She closed hers briefly with a look of horror and moved convulsively.

'It's all right,' he said quietly, adroitly clasping up her bra, running his fingers around its upper edges, then smoothing her jacket and buttoning it up and turning his head at the second, timid knock. 'Come in.'

It was the girl from the typing pool, Verity saw before she turned away hastily. Come to collect some papers she'd left, she said. On Mr Morris's desk, she added very apologetically, and yes, she could see them and she could just nip in and out and get them and leave them in *peace*. This she said with an unmistakable kind of significance and a hurried look at Verity, who had turned back, and then blushed.

'By all means,' Brad said pleasantly and sat down on the corner of Verity's desk.

She was as good as her word, except that she tripped on the way out, and if she'd looked embarrassed before it was nothing to how she looked as she closed the door.

Verity drew a deep, quivering breath and started to blush herself.

He smiled faintly and reached over and took her hand. 'Don't.'

She tried to pull it away and said tautly, 'Why not? It will be all over the office before you can say Jack Robinson!'

He grimaced. 'She actually saw nothing, Verity. Although she might have got the vibes,' he conceded. 'But who cares?'

'*I* care——'

'Why? It happened—to my mind the much more important thing is why it happened. I think we should discuss that, don't you?' He raised an eyebrow at her, his grey gaze alert and slightly quizzical, and he moved his fingers on the inside of her wrist.

To her horror, that action caused her to feel as if it was happening to her all over again—What is happening to me? she wondered frantically. 'You,' she licked her lips, '*you* caused it to happen, Mr Morris.' And gained momentum as a rather sick feeling invaded her and caused her to feel both frightened and angry. 'You must have a remarkably short memory if you don't recall that your hurt pride led you into an exercise of sheer male chauvinism!' And she snatched her wrist away.

His eyes narrowed. 'Well, now,' he drawled, and his gaze dropped to her breasts, 'is that how you always react to exercises of sheer male chauvinism, Mrs Wood? Or was I right all along? Have you starved yourself of love for reasons best known to yourself, and frustrated yourself in the process to the extent that you just couldn't help yourself? It's just as well we were interrupted then. Otherwise I could have had you on the floor, couldn't I?' He looked up at last and his eyes were a cool, mocking grey.

Verity went white, causing her freckles to be really noticeable and her eyes to look a dark, molten gold. She started to speak, swallowed, then said, 'Goodbye, Mr Morris. I'm resigning.' And she picked up her two bags then realised she was still boxed into a corner, in a manner of speaking, and she added through her teeth, 'Get out of my *way*, damn you!'

He did, unhurriedly.

CHAPTER TWO

'VERITY!'

'Hello, Mum.'

'What are you doing home this early in the day? Are you feeling sick, darling?'

Verity put her bags plus a plastic bag full of groceries on the kitchen table. 'No.' She sighed. 'I've quit.'

Her mother, who was small, grey-haired but chic and lively-looking, laid the letter she'd been reading down and stared at her daughter, open-mouthed. 'Why?'

Verity gestured. 'It's a long story. I've told you how difficult he is to work for. I just—blew my top today.' She flinched inwardly as she thought of all the other things she'd done, things she had no intention of revealing to her mother or to anyone else.

'Well, darling, yes, you have told me, but it's an extremely well-paid job and——'

'There are other jobs. In fact, I've had several approaches from other advertising firms, so—don't worry.' She smiled at her mother reassuringly. 'Where's Maddy?'

'Gone shopping with Tanya and her mother—it never rains but it pours,' Lucy Chalmers added vexedly.

'It's actually fine, and lovely outside,' Verity murmured, and started to put the groceries away.

'No, I mean *this*.' Lucy waved the letter she'd been reading agitatedly. 'It's from Helen. Would you believe, she's broken her ankle?'

Helen was Lucy's sister, Verity's aunt, a genuine spinster, Verity thought—perhaps because she had those thoughts rather prominently in mind—and headmistress of a country school. Who lived on her own, moreover, and would be seriously handicapped with a broken ankle, her thoughts ran on as she began to perceive the other cause of her mother's distress.

'Ah,' she said slowly. 'Well, it couldn't have worked out better. I can look after Maddy while you go and look after Auntie Helen. It really *couldn't* have worked out better, in fact!'

'Verity,' her mother looked at her seriously, 'you'll want to be out and about, looking for another job. I know you've done marvellously well financially, but there's still the rent to pay and the repayments on the car, the electricity bill came today, together with the telephone bill, and they're due on the same day—I don't know why, but they always are——'

Verity grimaced. 'I have got a bit put aside, Mum.'

Her mother looked supremely dubious; then she brightened. 'Look, I've thought of the perfect solution! I'll take Maddy with me. She'd love a little break in the country, and you do know she's as safe with me as she is with you!'

'Oh, Mum,' Verity looked at her with deep affection in her eyes, 'yes, and I don't know what I would have done without you, but . . . it'll be so much work—Maddy, and Auntie Helen with a broken ankle. No, no, I'll cope——'

'You will not, Verity Chalmers—sorry, Wood,' her mother said, drawing herself up to her full height, which was all of five feet two. 'I'm as strong as a horse anyway. And supposing you do find another job and they want you to start work straight away? What then? You'd have to put Maddy into a crèche of some kind—you know how I feel about that! No, this is the way we'll do it. You could even drive down to see us on the weekends—of course, you'll miss Maddy and she'll miss you, so that will solve that, and Helen would love to see you as well. Unless the Woods...?' Her mother stopped abruptly.

'They did not,' Verity said drily. 'Nothing has changed there. Mum,' she paused and bit her lip and considered that she really couldn't afford to be unemployed for very long, 'if you're really sure?'

Lucy relaxed. 'Of course I am, pet! Now tell me what Mr Morris did to upset you so greatly?'

Verity's face thinned and she was silent for a moment; then she grimaced and managed to say fairly lightly, 'I shouldn't know where to begin.'

'Well, he is a very clever man apparently. I mean, you just have to look at his ads, and then there's the journalism he does on the side—I love his travel column in the paper! It's so witty and different ... and didn't you tell me he writes school textbooks? Books with such an ingenious approach that kids just can't help understanding things better?'

'I have never tried to deny that he's clever, astonishingly versatile and a whole lot of other things, Mum. It doesn't alter the fact that he's quite impossible,' Verity said with finality.

That evening she persuaded her mother to go to the pictures with a friend. 'It might be your last chance for a while,' she said with a grin. Lucy was an avid film-goer, and all the arrangements for their departure the following day had been made. Once Lucy Chalmers made up her mind about anything, she was an amazingly fast worker, and Verity was to drive them down and spend one night with them.

'It will help to settle Maddy in,' she'd said, 'and give you a bit of a break, but then you really ought to get stuck into finding a job!'

Verity couldn't help smiling to herself as she and Maddy, who was bathed and in her pyjamas, did a jigsaw puzzle—or rather, Maddy concentrated fiercely on it. They were sitting on high stools at the kitchen counter and, although it was officially winter in Brisbane, no one had told the weather, and the front door of the small duplex was open to admit some balmy night air. They'd had dinner and there was a pot of coffee percolating gently on the stove, filling the place with its aroma. And Verity was smiling, despite her traumatic day, because not only was her mother an incredibly fast worker but also because she herself was incredibly lucky to have a mother like Lucy, whom Maddy adored and felt quite safe with.

She looked down and gently plucked one of her daughter's springy fine red-gold curls without breaking her concentration, and felt her heart contract as it so often did when she thought of the miracle that was Maddy. And she didn't know what alerted her, but after a moment or two something did, although she heard no sound, and she looked up and saw Brad Morris standing in the open front doorway.

She stayed arrested, a curl still wound round her finger, and felt suddenly suffused with a hot, blushing sense of shame. Then she released the curl and stood up. 'What do *you* want?'

Maddy looked up, wide-eyed, as he stepped over the doorstep into the lounge, then she turned and buried her face in Verity's loose-knit top. Verity picked her up. 'It's all right, honeybunch,' she said softly, regretting her harsh earlier tones but shooting Brad Morris an angry glance.

He stopped in the middle of lounge. Then he shook his head as if to clear it, and said, 'Why didn't you ever tell me?'

'It's got nothing to do with you,' Verity said stiffly.

'That you have a child? No,' he agreed, 'not *per se*, but I don't see why it should be such a deep, dark secret, either.'

'You did say, when you interviewed me, that it wasn't the kind of job that would suit anyone with encumbrances,' she reminded him with a bitter little smile.

He considered. 'It's not. You managed very well, all the same. But tell me, what other disinformation did you pass on? *Was* there ever a Mr Wood? I mean, are you a widow or a single parent?'

'Oh, there certainly was a Mr Wood,' Verity said with irony. 'And I am a widow and a single parent, as it happens, but be that as it may—what do you want?'

He stared at her and the child in her arms. 'What's her name? She's very shy, isn't she? But you must know, Verity,' he raised his grey eyes to hers, 'that I do not go about frightening children.'

It was all too true, Verity had to acknowledge. How he did it was something of a mystery; he certainly made no overt approaches, he wasn't a patter of heads or a pincher of cheeks, he offered no bribes, although he could do a few things that fascinated kids—but in fact he often indicated a lack of interest that one would have thought would turn them off. Yet it had the opposite effect. The only analogy that she'd been able to come up with was her own aversion to cats and the discovery that if you set out to ignore a cat it would be piqued enough to want to climb on to your lap and no one else's.

'She's more than shy,' Verity said abruptly.

'Oh? Why?'

Verity looked at him frustratedly. 'She doesn't trust men—not that it's anything——'

'To do with me,' he finished for her, and added with a faint smile, 'I wonder if she gets it from her mum? But look,' he went on before Verity could respond, 'why don't you put her down and let her finish her jigsaw, you can sit right next to her as you were, and we could ... continue our discussion?'

'There's nothing to discuss. *If* you've come to beg me to return——'

'I have,' he said blandly and wandered over to the counter, where he idly picked up a piece of jigsaw and after a moment fitted it into place. 'Not precisely beg, but point out the mutual benefits; that sort of thing.'

Verity was conscious of two things: the creeping knowledge that Brad Morris didn't ever give up, and the fact that Maddy had raised her head and was watching what he was doing interestedly. I might have known, she thought exasperatedly, and was further exasperated when Maddy suddenly indicated that she wanted to get back to her jigsaw. Verity put her down on the stool and avoided Brad's eyes.

'You haven't told me her name. Or why she doesn't trust me,' he said quietly.

'Her name is Madeleine. She's three, and that's all I intend to tell you, Mr Morris,' Verity replied equally quietly but with clear intent.

'All right,' he said mildly. 'Well, now she's settled, why don't you offer me a cup of coffee? I can assure you I could do with one. I have spent the entire afternoon with Len Pearson. I'm exhausted, wrung out, talked out, I haven't eaten—and, despite your conviction that I wouldn't personally do anything to return him to the fold, he is returned, and it was entirely due to my heroic efforts. Are these biscuits?' He picked up a barrel on the counter, opened it and sniffed appreciatively. 'Home-made shortbread, I do believe. Is that another of your talents, Verity? May I help myself?'

'My mother made them. Oh,' she muttered and turned away to the stove. 'One cup of coffee and then you leave,' she said as evenly as possible, and only for Maddy's sake.

'Of course.' He waited patiently, pulling himself up a stool and munching shortbread as if he really was starving. 'Thanks. By the way, I've changed my mind,' he said conversationally as she passed him a steaming mug and pushed milk and sugar towards him.

'Good. I'm surprised, but it would be impossible to go on——'

'Not about that. No, I've decided to give the red-headed twins a miss. I'm going to use a cockatoo instead, a talking one, naturally.'

Verity groaned then coloured.

He went on, waving a biscuit, 'Len Pearson gave me the idea actually. Did you know the man is a multi-millionaire and that he's recently started a charter-boat company in Port Douglas? You can hire his boats and everything is provided—skipper, crew, et cetera.'

'I know a great deal about Len Pearson and he knows a great deal about me,' Verity said a shade wearily. 'After all, I've spoken to him nearly every day for the last six weeks. He also owns a frozen-food empire, a sixty-foot yacht, his wife died a year ago, he's very lonely and he's been an amateur inventor for some time.'

Brad cocked an eyebrow. 'Has he been making telephonic passes at you, Verity? I must say, he was most disturbed to hear that we had—parted company. He more or less told me that unless I got you back he *would* take his account elsewhere.'

'As well as everything else, he is sixty-two,' Verity pointed out acidly. 'And I thought you said you had got him back——'

'That was never a safeguard against anything— being sixty-two——'

'*Mr* Morris——' Verity bit her lip as Maddy moved restlessly then yawned.

'Looks like bedtime to me,' Brad murmured. 'And not *before* time,' he said with a charming smile, 'if you intend to get all heated again, Verity. May I make some shadow faces on the wall for her before she goes? I've added a new one to my repertoire. Let me show you.'

The net result, and it was all about as flattening as an encounter with a steamroller, was that Maddy went to bed charmed and delighted and fell asleep almost as soon as her head touched the pillow.

And by the time Verity returned to the kitchen Brad had freshened their coffee.

'Where was I? Ah, yes, we were discussing Len Pearson, but if that's a painful subject we could get on to the cockatoo——'

'No. Look here,' Verity said, 'I'm not coming back.'

'Mr Morris,' he drawled.

She blinked at him.

'You forgot to say it in that frozen way you usually do, that's all. Why?'

Verity took a deep breath and took refuge in her coffee for a moment. 'I must be slipping, Mr Morris,' she said drily then.

'I meant, why won't you come back, Verity?'

'I should have thought that was obvious,' she said shortly.

'Well, it's not, actually. By the way, I haven't entirely given up on redheads. I would also like to include a red-bearded, kilted, bagpipe-playing Scotsman and a boat—as well as a talking cockatoo.'

'Isn't that a bit hackneyed?' Verity said before she could stop herself. 'I mean, people have been making fun of kilted Scotsmen for—a long time probably.'

He sat forward. 'That's what you don't understand. So few do! It's those wonderful, hackneyed things that people love . . . Mind you,' he sat back reflectively, 'I have had other ideas. I have this image of a mediocrely pretty woman but one of those incredibly tenacious ones with all the mediocre ambitions in life—tiled patios around bungalows, cooking in woks, fondue parties—and the kind of woman who persists in calling her husband Douglas or Richard or Michael when everyone else, their mothers included, calls them Doug or Dick or Mick.'

'That's diabolical,' Verity said slowly, but she couldn't help smiling. 'On the whole, I prefer the Scot.'

'Do you know any?'

'No. Anyway——'

'Verity, can I tell you something else?' he queried and proceeded to do so. 'Len Pearson is contemplating a major *international* advertising drive for his frozen foods as well as something for this fleet of charter boats that takes tourists to the Barrier Reef from Port Douglas. But, being no fool, he's not prepared to part with his hard-earned dollars on any old campaign, he wants the best, so he's come up with this—test drive, you might call it, on his own ... quite clever little invention, and I *refuse* to laud it any further.' He grimaced. 'But the gist of the thing is, get this one right and we get the other two. How,' he looked at her earnestly, 'could you possibly even consider deserting the camp at a time like this? Have you any idea what it will mean to the Morris Advertising Agency? The frozen-food one alone is like manna from heaven. It's already a household name—all we'll have to do is jazz up its image slightly and the——'

'Don't go on,' Verity said quietly. 'There is nothing so indispensable about me that will make or break this campaign, so you're wasting your time playing on my finer feelings, it's just ridiculous!'

'It's not. You yourself put it all in a nutshell only today. I'll be lost! Do you have any idea how many people I interviewed before I came up with you? Do you imagine I would have been half or even a quarter as productive as I've been over the past two years if it hadn't been for you? How many people do *you* know who can come up with a cockatoo, a red-bearded, kilted, bagpipe-playing Scotsman and a boat without all *sorts* of fuss and then keep us all happy into the bargain——?'

'Even I might have trouble with that,' Verity said drily.

'The cockatoo or the Scotsman?'

'Both.'

'Verity——'

'Mr Morris, I hesitate to say this, but why are you deliberately ignoring what happened this morning? If it demonstrates nothing else, surely it does demonstrate that our days of being able to work together so productively,' she said ironically, 'are gone?'

He eyed her alertly. 'I wasn't sure that you'd want that resurrected,' he said after a moment.

'Believe me, I don't. I——'

'By the way, I do apologise for the "having you on the floor" bit. That was unforgivable, not to mention horribly ungallant.'

Verity felt the warmth stealing into her cheeks but resolutely ignored it. 'And the next time it happens? Will you be able to refrain from being horribly ungallant again? And again?' she said gently.

He looked at her thoughtfully, then raised an eyebrow. 'If you don't kiss me back the next time, I might.'

Her fingers curved about her coffee-mug, but she restrained herself and said in a colourless voice, 'There will be no next time—that's what I'm trying to tell you.'

He looked her over in silence, taking in her slim yellow trousers and loose white cotton top, her flat yellow shoes and absence of any make-up, which was as informally dressed as he'd ever seen her, then said with a faint frown, 'Do you honestly think you were entirely blameless this morning, Verity?' He gestured with a tinge of irritation. 'Blame is not the right word, but you know what I mean.'

She closed her eyes. 'I don't want to discuss it. It *happened*, and it makes it impossible for us to work together; that's all there is to say.'

'What about anything else?'

She opened her eyes. 'What about it? What else?'

'Well, you seem to be seriously suggesting that, although it *happened*, we pretend it didn't—we ignore it, in other words. Yet I can assure you, for all my sins, I don't normally go around doing that kind of thing willy-nilly.' He smiled without amusement. 'Nor, I'm equally sure, do you. Not,' he added quietly, 'as passionately as we did it, Verity.'

It was a moment before Verity spoke, and it took a great deal of will-power to not only frame an answer when she would have preferred to fall through a handy hole in the floor, but also to utter it with a semblance of composure. 'I think,' she said slowly, 'we will just have to put it down to being one of those mysterious things that can be neither explained nor should be...agonised over. That's what I really think, Mr Morris.' She raised her golden eyes to his and there was a kind of bleak defiance in them. Then she couldn't help adding with some irony, 'What, as a matter of interest, do you think Miss Carpenter would have made of it all?'

His mouth hardened. 'Let's leave Primrose out of this, Verity. It——'

'Oh, I see,' she mocked, and their gazes locked in a way that was about as combative as two people could get without coming to blows—which gave Verity a curious sense of satisfaction. Got you there, Mr Morris, she thought.

But he merely said with a flash of something in his eyes that was gone before it was decipherable, 'I doubt if you do see, but if that's how you really feel then all more the reason for us *not* to break up a wonderfully successful *working* relationship all because of a—what would you call it?—a non-event, really. Particularly as I intend to offer you a rise, and a further one if we get Pearson's other account and——'

'Mr Morris——'

'I *wish* you wouldn't keep calling me that,' he said, really irritably this time. 'And may I make another point? We've been discussing this for,' he consulted his watch, 'an hour now, during which time neither of us has shown any inclination to leap on the other and none of that naughtiness of the *non-event* kind has surfaced at all. Or has it?' he challenged, looking every bit as autocratic and unamused and wildly impatient as only he could.

Verity opened her mouth to deny that it had, but her mother chose that moment to walk in.

Verity groaned inwardly then said to Lucy, who had stopped in the kitchen with a surprised expression, 'This is Mr Morris, Mum. He's just leaving,' she added flatly.

'Oh, please don't leave on my account, Mr Morris,' Lucy said hastily. 'I'm quite ready for bed, actually. I've just seen this *exhausting* movie. No, do stay and talk to Verity. Especially,' she said, taking Verity supremely by surprise, 'if you've come to talk her into staying with you.'

The result was entirely predictable. Brad Morris slid off his stool and advanced upon her mother, exuding the charm he could also turn on like no other from every pore. 'I can't tell you how delighted I am to meet you, ma'am! And I do hope you'll forgive me, but I've eaten just about all your absolutely delicious biscuits, and I *am* here to talk Verity into coming back, but I'm having little success.'

'Ah,' Lucy said, and subjected Brad to a penetrating scrutiny, and it was obvious from what she then said that she approved of what she saw. She said, 'Between you and me, Mr Morris, Verity can be a very determined person sometimes. However, I see that as a character asset, on the whole.'

'So do I,' Brad agreed ruefully.

'Had you, then, considered apologising to her for whatever it was you fell out over? Or perhaps promising to mend your ways somewhat?' she queried a little sternly. 'All Verity has told me is that you're . . . just impossible.' Her expression relented slightly as she added, 'Men so often simply don't realise they are, you know.'

For just a second Brad Morris stared at her, transfixed, and was without words. Then he swung around to Verity so that only she could see the little glint in his eye as he said very seriously, 'I apologise for *everything*, Verity. And I shall certainly try to mend my ways.'

'Now, Verity, it would be churlish not to at least allow Mr Morris a probationary period,' Lucy Chalmers said gently to her daughter. 'Wouldn't it?'

'Darling, are you still cross with me?'

'No,' Verity said and changed gear.

'Because I talked you into going back to work for Mr Morris?'

'Mum, I've just said I'm not cross with you.'

'Unfortunately I know you well enough to know that you're annoyed about something!' Lucy said humorously and glanced over to the back seat to see how Maddy was. 'But I found him quite charming—oh, I'm sure he can be difficult. I mean, you can *see* the energy and the intelligence—I wouldn't be surprised if the air literally hums about him at times.'

Verity winced and changed down again.

'But I really couldn't help feeling that you have *great* prospects with him. After all, considering how inexperienced you were in advertising when he hired you, he's already done great things for you, and, well, the devil you know, especially one who pays you as well as he does and proposes to pay you even *more...*' She didn't finish that bit but started on another thought. 'Besides which, you like advertising, don't you? I mean, you find it interesting and challenging and would like to make it your career, and, from what I've read, Brad Morris is about *the* most exciting person in the game today. Did he make a pass at you, Verity?'

Verity turned her head to study her mother briefly, then sighed. 'Something of that nature occurred, yes,' she conceded formally. 'How did you guess?'

Her mother chuckled. 'Why do one's offspring always imagine one came down with the last shower, particularly in romantic matters? Were you being very superior, dear? About men in general or something like that?'

Verity was silent.

'Well, I won't probe any further,' Lucy said brightly. 'But I do think one should forgive men the odd pass from time to time. I mean, it obviously couldn't have been the ongoing, obnoxious, bottom-pinching kind of thing or you'd have left ages ago. I would take it as a compliment if I were you. They just can't help themselves occasionally, even nice ones, you know, poor dears. And you should also bear in mind that you're a bit sensitive on the subject of men, anyway. Not without cause,' her mother said soberly. 'But not all men are like *that*.'

Verity drove for a while in silence, then she glanced at her mother and smiled wryly. 'You're so sane. I'm sorry I've been like a bear with a sore head.'

'Didn't you tell me he has this fabulous girlfriend?' Lucy said relievedly.

'Yes. Primrose Carpenter. She's that model I pointed out to you in a magazine. They've been together for quite a while now. As long as I've worked for him—at least, I've been sending her flowers and chocolates and all sorts of wild and wonderful things since I started working for him.'

'What kind of wild and wonderful things?' Lucy asked with a laugh.

'Well, I told you about the giant panda bear—toy, of course—then there was the bicycle made for two and,' Verity paused, 'as a matter of fact, a talking *cockatoo* . . .'

Lucy laughed again. 'He does sound like an exciting person to be in love with. Will they marry, do you think?'

'I think it's only a question of when.'

Lucy pursed her lips. 'She might be wise to get him to the altar sooner rather than later.'

Verity had to smile herself. 'To curb these outbreaks of—whatever it is even nice men can't help from time to time? You could be right. I think we're here.'

Her mother squeezed her arm fondly. 'That's my girl. You look much better now.'

But that night in bed, with Maddy snuggled up to her, and even with the comforting knowledge that Maddy had taken to her Great-Aunt Helen's country establishment like a duck to water—there were some ducklings and chickens, a lamb and a kitten, all of which had fascinated her—Verity didn't feel much better, she discovered. In fact, there seemed to be an aching little void around her heart that, much as she wished to, she couldn't solely attribute to missing Maddy, as she undoubtedly would. And she dared not, she found, allow herself to dwell on what other causes there might be for it.

CHAPTER THREE

IT WAS, two days later, impossible to be unaware of the discreet buzz of speculation as Verity arrived for work. Not only had she to run the gauntlet of the receptionist and an unusually large number of employees in Reception, but she also ran into both Tim Cameron and William Morris on the way to Brad's suite of offices.

Tim was looking more his usual urbane self, and he said heartily, 'Great to see you, Mrs Wood! So glad you changed your mind.'

William Morris, however, drew her aside. 'Mrs Wood,' he began earnestly, 'I can't tell you how glad I am to see you. And I'm only sorry that I didn't take the opportunity to tell you, before—er—your little run-in with Brad, how much we value you at the Morris Advertising Agency. Not to put too fine a point on it, you've coped with Brad admirably, better than anyone else we've ever had, and at this point in time, with the prospect of the Pearson account tripling itself, it would be a disaster to lose you.'

'Thank you, Mr Morris,' Verity murmured.

'I'd also like to say, if you,' he gestured uncomfortably, 'have any more problems with Brad, please do come to me with them. I'm sure that between us we could sort them out!'

Verity controlled an insane desire to laugh hysterically as she visualised herself telling this staid, middle-aged man, who was so different from his brother, the exact nature of what had occurred between her and Brad Morris. 'Thank you,' was all she could find to say again.

'He's not...a *bad* person, really,' William persevered. 'In fact, the main problem is he's just been too darned bright for his own good ever since he was born, virtually. He exhausted our poor mother, who was always convinced he would come to a bad end; as a child at school...well, let's just say he exhausted them too, several of them. But we'd be a bit lost here without him. My wife...' He paused and grimaced, and Verity was assailed suddenly by Brad's 'mediocrely pretty woman' with pretensions who could have been Gloria Morris to a T, although of course she didn't have to confine herself to bungalows or cooking in woks now, and who couldn't, it was a well known fact, tolerate her brother-in-law. 'My wife,' William repeated, 'has always maintained he needs a really good woman to sort him out. My own opinion is that she would need to be a cross between a saint and a brigadier-general, but perhaps that's what Gloria means,' he reflected with a sudden look of surprise. 'Anyway, do remember I'm always available, Mrs Wood.'

'I will, Mr Morris.'

Consequently, as Verity entered the office, with curious visions of Brad Morris as an energetic, uncontrollable schoolboy in her mind, it came as even more of a shock to find her boss sitting behind his desk in an upright position, something he rarely did, and dressed in a neat dark suit, a pristine white shirt and a conservative royal-blue tie, which looked suspiciously like an old school tie—a quite famous old school tie, she recognised as she came closer.

She raised an eyebrow and couldn't help smiling faintly.

'Good morning, Verity,' he said promptly, and added, 'What, may one enquire, is the cause of your mirth?'

'Hardly mirth,' she responded, and turned away to her desk.

'You're surprised to see me dressed like this?'

'I am indeed. I'm more surprised by the tie, however.'

He grimaced. 'It's my old school tie—did you imagine I was born fully educated?'

'Not at all. But I have just been given to understand you—er—well, exhausted several schools as well as your poor mother, which led me to believe that you mightn't be a rightful recipient of an old school tie.'

Brad Morris lay back in his chair and looked entirely unperturbed. 'I did have a few changes but that was in my primary days,' he conceded. 'Who passed on all this startling information?'

Verity shrugged, sat down and began repacking her drawers from her shopping bag.

'It had to be Bill.' He chuckled. 'What else did he say?'

Verity shrugged evasively again.

'I see. Well, if you're wondering why I'm dressed the way I am, there are two reasons: I'm trying to reform, as I promised your delightful mother, and I thought therefore that looking the part of an advertising executive could only help me to act like one; and I'm meeting my publisher for lunch. You're looking very smart yourself, incidentally.'

Verity was wearing a straight, soft jade-green dress with a matching jacket—all very simple but well cut—with bronze accessories. 'Thanks,' she said briefly without looking up.

'How is Maddy?' Lucy had confided quite a few details to him at their legendary meeting, including their plans for the next few weeks.

'Fine.'

'I see,' he said again, and when she did glance up at last it was to see him looking perfectly serious, except for his grey eyes, which were glinting with amusement.

And she cautioned herself suddenly against over-reacting and said much against her will, 'She's settled in really well, actually. My aunt has a small menagerie of young animals and I shall be amazed if she doesn't come home with a kitten at least. Talking of animals or those kind of things,' she opened a fresh notebook and wrote 'Pearson Account', then raised her golden-flecked eyes to Brad Morris, 'are you still of the same mind? Regarding Scotsmen, cockatoos and boats?'

'I am.' He looked at her a little more narrowly. 'Have *you* been clobbered with inspiration?'

'Not precisely. But it did occur to me that only six months ago you gave Miss Carpenter a talking cockatoo—I remember it because I actually found it for you and it was a magnificent specimen. I wondered if she'd mind—lending it to us for the ad?'

'Ah.' Brad Morris drummed his long fingers thoughtfully on the desk for a moment, then said un-usually laconically, 'No.'

Verity couldn't help looking surprised. 'Did it die? Or fly away? Or stop talking?'

'None of those things. Well, it will soon be common knowledge, I suppose,' he said drily, 'but the fact of the matter is, Verity, that I've been thrown over for a member of the English aristocracy—no less than an earl,' and for a fleeting moment his eyes were hard and grim.

Verity stared at him, open-mouthed, until she reminded herself of the girl from the typing pool. But even then all she could say feebly was, 'What?'

'It's true.'

'But—I mean—only days ago you were . . .'

'That was our swan-song.' He sat back, the grimness replaced now by a deliberate kind of lazy world-weariness. 'Primrose and I—well, put it this way, Primmy was a bit undecided for a while. It is a giant leap forward for her, but she had some reservations; one would be a fool not to be aware that any aristocracy doesn't take too kindly to losing their earls to models, especially with Australian accents, however beautiful, but in the end she decided she had every attribute to be the Countess of So-and-So and to go for it. She has gone,' he added succinctly.

'But—you *let* her?' Verity was still having trouble with her voice and a tendency to look shell-shocked.

A definite look of irony crossed Brad's eyes before he remarked, 'Talented as I am, indeed, everything that I am, I'm still a long way from being a peer of the realm.'

'You could be as unhappy as the Countess of So-and-So as anyone else,' Verity said slowly as, for the first time in nearly two years, she tried to look into Brad Morris's soul and discover how he *really* felt. 'I mean, if you love each other and——'

'Verity, Verity,' he drawled. 'Are you that naïve? Let me explain the real dilemma of truly beautiful women to you. I mean that kind of matchless beauty that you see quite rarely, and you'd have to agree Primmy has it?' He raised an eyebrow at her.

'Yes. Yes, of course,' Verity agreed, trying not to sound even faintly tart.

'Well, it's their everything, you see. It's their entrée into all sorts of society, it can be a substitute for brains, although I wouldn't say Primmy was brainless, but it's such an asset above all else that they'd be...foolish if they didn't seek and strive for the right setting for it, didn't find a place for it where it could be cosseted and treasured and receive the right amount of exposure, which is like a form of nourishment to truly beautiful women—believe me, she'll never be quite as unhappy as the Countess of So-and-So, whatever he's like, as she could be looking back and thinking of what she *might* have been.'

Verity opened her mouth, hesitated, then said uncertainly, 'Have you any idea how cynical that sounds?'

He shrugged. 'I think it's a fact of life.'

Verity was silent beneath the weight of her thoughts—the sudden memory of the way he and Primrose had looked only a few days ago in this very room, the...yes, she reflected, the tension that had flowed between them, albeit briefly, and then the affection and tenderness in his eyes that he'd not been able to hide, the totally impossible mood he'd been in, even for him. And she remembered that fighting glance they'd exchanged and what he'd said when she'd mentioned Primrose that same evening and implied that he was being faithless if nothing else, and her unspoken surprise, unspoken even to herself, that Brad Morris was that kind of man... Why didn't he tell me then? she wondered. Because even the fact that he can't have her doesn't change the fact that he loves her? Of course... He didn't deny it just now, he embarked instead on what had to be a bitter and cynical discourse, even though he tried to make light of it...

Her eyes widened as it crossed her mind to wonder then whether the kiss they'd exchanged had been the unforgivable but perhaps only human reaction of a man who had been passed over for a peer of the realm?

'What,' he murmured, 'is crossing your mind, Verity?'

She blinked and coloured slightly, then raised her eyebrows at him with some hauteur. 'I'm surprised you can't read my mind. You seem to have set yourself up as quite an authority on women.'

'You don't think I'm right about Primrose?' he queried.

'I...' She stopped and started again. 'I would rather not go into it any further. How am I to know anyway?' she added crossly.

He shrugged. 'I got the distinct impression you were speculating, all the same.'

'No—that is to say, it's futile for me *to* speculate. *All right*,' she added to his look of scepticism, 'let's say I was human enough to do so briefly——'

'I would have thought you more than anyone would be in the position to speculate.'

Verity stared at him. Then she said, 'I'll tell you what position I am in, Mr Morris. One of being able to end the bargain we made any time I choose. So now either we drop the subject and get back to

business or I leave. Where were we? Ah, yes: cockatoos, painful a subject as they may be——'

'They aren't.'

Want to bet? Verity said, but to herself, and wrote
down 'Cockatoo' on her pad, and thought, Perhaps
I could borrow someone else's? I've got the feeling if
I buy one I'll be landed with it, and anyway, as I know
from previous experience, it's not that easy to buy
talking cockatoos... Then she raised her head as the
silence lengthened, to see her boss staring at her
broodingly.

'Is something wrong?' she asked involuntarily. 'I
mean, something else?'

His expression didn't change for a moment, then
he looked at her with such sardonic amusement that
she took a startled breath. But, before she had a
chance to say anything, he sat up. 'We have to go to
Port Douglas to make this ad, Verity. I don't know
if I mentioned it, but it should only take a week at
the most, unless *everything* goes wrong, so it won't
interfere with your visits to Maddy, but if we do get
caught up there over a weekend I will naturally give
you time off to compensate. We'll be going up by
train, the *Queenslander*, which will kill two birds with
one stone for me, and we'll fly home. So far as boats
go, one of the reasons for us going to Port Douglas
is that Len Pearson happens to have a plethora of
them up there—and he was rather charmed at the
thought that we might be able to use one of his boats,
thereby giving that area of his operations some free
publicity as well as establishing a link between his
commercial operations and his inventive genius. He
has also decided to start off the campaign on his
charter boats in a poster and pamphlet form, so we'll

be able to do the photography at the same time—thereby killing another two birds with one stone,' he said wryly. 'The Scotsman I'll have to leave up to you, Verity. If necessary, we can take one with us, but I think I'd rather find a local. You have three days to organise it. How does that suit you?'

Verity again closed her mouth, but this time she threw her notebook on to her desk and stood up, her eyes a deep molten gold. 'It doesn't,' she said crisply. 'How long have you known all this?' she demanded.

'Since I spent an exhausting afternoon with Len Pearson. I had to make some reparation for your damning comments, such as conceding, against my better judgement, as a matter of fact, Verity, that Port Douglas would be a good place to do all this—the man is simply fanatical about the place and he is paying so——'

'And you didn't see fit to tell me all this that *evening*? In other words, you lured me back under false pretences, Mr Morris——'

'I wondered when we'd get back to that,' he drawled.

'Did you?' she shot back at him. 'Well, now you know. And here's something else for you to know! I have no intention of spending weeks away with you, let alone being closeted on a train with you for *days*, so——'

'What are you frightened of, Verity?' he said softly but with a significant look. 'Yourself?'

She picked up the notebook and threw it at him. He dodged it lazily and eyed her quizzically, which incensed her all the more.

'There's nothing I'm frightened of,' she spat at him. 'What I object to is your incredible thoughtlessness, your unbelievably high-handed ways—"you have three days to organise it all, Verity",' she mimicked. 'Port Douglas has to be at least a *thousand* miles away! How the hell am I to know what facilities they have up there? Or whether there are any wandering Scots minstrels up there?' she said witheringly, and added, 'If you must know, the mere *thought* of kilts and bagpipes is starting to give me the heebie-jeebies, but, that aside, it could be an absolute nightmare trying to organise things up there, especially *your* kind of…things, which are inevitably a nightmare anyway! Why can't you just do something *simple* and close to home?' she said passionately. 'Why does it always have to be these three-ring-kind-of-circus deals?'

He took his time about answering, time he spent examining her extreme state of agitation, including her heaving breasts. Then he said mildly, 'I thought I'd explained why, but, that apart, anyone can do simple, ordinary things close to home. My inspiration comes from a much wider source, which is why my ads are such works of art. We have also been away from home, before, Verity, not to mention the fact that you haven't got anyone *at* home at the moment. And short notice has never been a problem before— that's how I work.'

'Your modesty is also unbelievable,' she ground out, and sat down with a disgusted sound. 'Three days,' she marvelled. 'No. I refuse to do it. I don't choose to be that *far* away from home anyway.'

'You didn't make any such stipulations when you agreed to come back to work.'

'I didn't *know* you were planning to turn this into an extended safari——'

'So it would have affected your decision?' he queried, with a lazy glint in his eye that should have warned her but didn't.

'Yes,' she said shortly.

'Then I think the events that passed between us several days ago have to be the cause,' he said with the sort of lazy mockery that was equally stinging as the more overt kind. 'You've never before objected to my *modus operandi*, you see.'

Verity took a furious breath. 'And *I* can't help thinking Primrose Carpenter is well shot of you, you know. I'm sure even an earl would find it difficult to have an ego as large as yours! Had you taken that into consideration, Mr Morris? That you might have actually sent her flying into the arms of her earl because you are such a monumental egotist?'

Apart from the knowledge that she'd been possessed of an unbelievable desire to wound him or his vanity or something, and had given way to it in an unforgivably personal manner—and it struck her as soon as the words left her mouth—she was almost immediately assailed then by the knowledge that she might as well be hitting her head against a brick wall. Because he made no movement but sat there studying her with nothing more than a little glint of curiosity in his eyes, as if viewing with a sort of universal cynicism now yet another genre of the female species— not, she couldn't doubt it, the *truly* beautiful type, but probably the hysterical, bitchy type . . . She raised her hands to her face frustratedly.

Then, at last, he sat forward and said meditatively, 'Verity, I've got the feeling some man made your life hell once, and *I* can't help speculating that it might have been the late, possibly *unlamented* Mr Wood.'

She took her hands away. Then she took several very deep breaths and said tonelessly, 'Would you please explain why it's necessary to go up there by train? If what I've read is true, it takes two days and a night.'

His eyes narrowed and for a moment he looked as if he was in two minds, but perhaps the bleak, cold look in her eyes helped him to decide. He said, drily, however, 'The paper I write for wants me to do a series of articles on Australian trains, starting with the *Queenslander*. It occurred to me that at the same time it might be a very peaceful way to—finalise my ideas on Len Pearson's thingumajig.' He started to look irritated and picked up one of Len Pearson's 'thingumajigs', actually called a Kneg, from the desk, and stared down at it so balefully that it suddenly occurred to Verity that this ad was causing her brilliant boss some problems.

'I rarely doubt myself,' he continued, 'but how anyone can get so worked up over a fiddling sort of cross between a clothes-peg and a penknife is enough to make me start. Anyone would think he'd invented the original safety-pin!'

'Ah, but,' Verity said, 'if you were a Scotsman caught on a windy boat who had lost his safety-pin but not his penknife, it could be a lifesaver.'

'Verity!' For a moment he looked totally entertained—indeed, he looked so vitally alive that it caused her heart to contract in a manner that was acutely disturbing. 'You've read my mind!'

'I have had a bit of practice,' she said as prosaically as she was able. 'As a matter of fact, it is quite a useful little thing, and it did occur to me that it might have some impact if it *didn't* have a name. I mean, perhaps you could devise three or four scenarios instead of just the one, where someone who doesn't know what it is finds it useful in bizarre circumstances then looks at it perplexedly and asks what it really is. And then you could flash the name across the screen with a sort of "don't leave home without one" message.'

There was dead silence for a long moment, during which Verity started to feel uncomfortable and as if she'd overstepped her mark or suggested something stupid to say the least, and she grimaced and murmured, 'Not terribly original, probably—it was just a thought.'

'My dear,' he said softly, but his grey eyes sparkled magnetically, 'I don't know why I'm sitting in this chair instead of you. Unoriginal be damned—it's brilliant!' He frowned. 'Why didn't I think of it?' he demanded. 'I've been racking my brains for bloody weeks!'

'Perhaps you had other things on your mind. And you did come up with the Scotsman,' she consoled him.

'So I did.' He grimaced, then brightened. 'This calls for a celebration. I'm taking you out to lunch, Verity, whether you like it or not,' he said with all his old assurance, and stood up.

She sighed and struggled to keep a straight face. 'It's only nine-thirty in the morning, Mr Morris,' she pointed out gently. 'Besides, you're lunching with your publisher.'

He glanced at his watch, pursed his lips and sat down again. 'That's true—tell you what, though, you'd enjoy meeting my publisher, so I shall still take you out to lunch. But in the meantime, could you get me Len Pearson on the phone, please? If he invented the thing he must have some idea of all the bizarre uses it can be put to.' And he pulled a pad towards him, which happened to be the one she'd thrown at him, read what she'd written, glanced across at her with a wicked little glint in his eye, then tossed it back gently so that it landed fair and square in front of her. 'Put the damned cockatoo on hold,' he said. 'You're right, I've suddenly decided I'm allergic to them.'

An hour later such was the level of activity in the office that Verity was quite confident that her boss would completely forget about his lunch invitation, if not the lunch itself. She was wrong.

At twelve-thirty he looked at his watch, reached for his jacket and tie, which he had discarded, ran a hand through his disordered hair and said to everyone in the office, 'That's it, folks. I'm taking my assistant out to lunch. Ready, Verity? You can titivate at the restaurant if necessary.'

His brother William, who had been made privy to the latest developments in the ongoing saga of the Pearson account, and who was looking pleased and genial, suddenly looked even more pleased and genial. 'What a good idea!' he enthused. 'Don't rush back, you two. I'll draft someone from my office to do a bit more of the groundwork for you, Mrs Wood.'

'This is unnecessary,' Verity said as they left the building. 'What could I possibly have in common with your publisher?'

He looked down at her amusedly. 'That's one of the delights of life, surely? You never know what you're going to have in common with strangers, do you? But you will have one thing: your sex.'

'She's a woman—I might have known,' Verity muttered.

'Now why would you say that, I wonder?' he queried as they stopped at a traffic-light. 'Or have you really decided I'm a womaniser of the worst kind, given,' he remarked quite audibly, 'to taking serious disadvantage of my assistant whenever the mood takes me? I notice,' he added with a significant downward glance, 'that you're wearing the kind of clothes it would not be so easy to slide my hands beneath today, Mrs Wood. From the top, that is.'

There were about six people around them at the junction but they all exhibited the same reaction— quick, disbelieving sidelong glances and then deliberately blank expressions.

Verity tightened her mouth and refused to budge when the light changed until everyone had moved on. Then she said as she started to walk, 'You fight incredibly dirty, don't you?'

He shrugged. 'I—retaliate, yes. And I guess I'll keep doing it while you continue to hold this distorted view of me, my motives and *your* total lack of involvement.'

'You also apologised for everything once—how false was that?' she marvelled.

'As a matter of fact, I thought you were far too intelligent to go on believing I *could* apologise for some things.'

Verity looked up at him and was a little stunned to see that he looked reticent and reserved, not mocking nor even amused, and that as he loped along, instead of looking incongruous in his beautifully tailored suit, there was something dynamic and intensely masculine about him, something completely at home, and it was not lost on most of the women walking towards him—they were even giving him backward glances. But, for reasons buried too deep for her to take into account, she continued to fight.

'I don't know how you can—I mean, if you still wish to harp on what happened, as you obviously do, may I present it to you in another light? Primrose had not even *gone* when you...when you——'

'When I succumbed to the intense attraction that was flowing between us that day, Verity?' he supplied, stopping in the middle of the pavement. 'Ah, but you see, I'd known Primmy was a lost cause for quite a few weeks. I was merely being a good friend in need while we were away. Also, contrary to your belief that it was an idyll for two in the Whitsundays, we were, in fact, part of a group, and *I* was working, hard as you may find that to believe as well, but if you care to read the Saturday paper for the next few weeks you could even find yourself quite entertained by my lively, witty, utterly refreshing view of the Whitsundays, which had been done to death in sheer banality by everyone else. We're here,' he added gravely.

The restaurant was small but beautifully appointed, and when he suggested a drink at the bar while they waited for his publisher to arrive she excused herself instead and looked around for the powder-room.

'Over there,' he pointed. 'Don't try to leave by the fire escape, Verity. That would be rather craven, don't you agree?'

What amazed her as she rinsed her hands and stared at her reflection in the mirror was how well she looked.

A seething state of anger must have subtle but beneficial properties, she reflected as she touched up her make-up, and decided it was more a matter of aura than actual looks. Because her hair usually shone and held its bouffant short shape with a fringe with no more than a flick of a comb—it was that kind of obliging hair—her skin was usually smooth and golden with its bloom of freckles, and her figure beneath the elegant jade outfit had not altered a centimetre in any direction. So why? she wondered. I mean, why should I look as if I've spent all morning preparing for this lunch instead of looking harassed and hard-worked? Why should I look clear-eyed and alert and as fresh as a daisy? Could it be that I was beginning to...*feel* dull and a bit deadly, and Brad Morris, if nothing else, has shaken me out of it? She grimaced, then looked at herself very soberly and said softly, 'Keep fighting, Verity. Don't let him wear you down, and above all it might be wise to remember that passive resistance could be more helpful to you than—the other kind.'

A few minutes later it struck her as rather ironic that his publisher of all people should be instrumental in helping her to continue the fight.

And it was obvious that Sonia Mallory was as surprised to see her as the opposite was true.

'So you two know each other?' Brad said as they sat down. 'I told you you might have something in common with each other,' he added to Verity.

Sonia, who was in her late thirties and one of those very refined, elegant women, although obviously with a sharp brain beneath it all, said languidly, 'Verity was married to my cousin Barry. You must have met Barry, Brad. You went to the same school, although he was years behind you—well, perhaps he missed you—he would have been only... twenty-five now, Verity?' She looked at Verity for confirmation.

'Yes.'

'Ah,' Brad murmured. 'No, I don't remember him, but——' he too turned to Verity '—you didn't tell me you were one of *those* Woods, Verity!'

There was a short, sharp silence. Then Verity said with commendable restraint, 'Only by marriage. And they didn't approve of me, so I don't claim any kinship.'

Sonia grimaced. 'I have to say, Verity,' she commented, 'that I always felt his parents—my uncle and aunt—did go out on a rather extraordinary limb over you, my dear, but it was such a very *young* marriage that surely, in retrospect, you can see their point? It wasn't terribly successful, after all, was it?'

Verity picked up the glass of wine that had just been poured for her and stared down into its golden depths for a moment before she said, 'If that was all they'd had against me, yes, I have to say, if nothing else, history proved them correct. But there was much more to it, Sonia. From the moment they laid eyes on me they decided I wasn't good enough for Barry; they never once considered that *he* might not have been good marriage material for *anyone*; they never ever acknowledged that he had a serious drinking problem—yes,' she said as Sonia's eyes widened, 'I wondered how much they'd played that down, but it was one he acquired before he met me, and somehow or other he managed to hide it from me as well until it was too late.'

Some doubt expressed itself in her late-husband's cousin's eyes, and it was because of that that Verity decided to continue, 'And it was the ridiculous pressure they put on him over me that exacerbated it. They also refused me any kind of help when I needed it desperately, they cut him out of their wills and told him it would stay that way so long as he stayed married to me—of course, the awful irony of that was Barry predeceasing them both and dying virtually penniless and with not a cent to pass on to his child, their only grandchild. And finally they virtually accused me of *driving* him to drink and thereby driving himself into a tree. Oh,' she said gently and put the wine down, untasted, 'one last thing—they do want to help with Maddy now, they've decided. I got a summons several days ago—do you know how they put it, Sonia? They told me that, in return for specified amounts of time she spent with them, they would be prepared to contribute to her schooling.'

Brad, who had been following all this with a growing frown in his eyes, said suddenly, 'Was that the morning you took off work? The day I got back?'

Verity looked at him sardonically. 'None other.'

'But why weren't you good enough for him?' he asked.

'If anyone should understand that, *you* should,' Verity said.

'No. No, I don't,' he murmured, the light of obstinacy that she was all too familiar with entering his grey eyes.

Verity waited until their meals had been served, during which time she debated whether to go on with this conversation, let alone the lunch, then decided she might as well be in for a pound as well as a penny. 'The English aren't the only ones who have an aristocracy. There's one right here in Brisbane and they generally live in Ascot or Hamilton, or that's where their parents live, and they too don't take too kindly to surrendering their sons, even if they aren't earls, to girls who didn't go to the right schools, who had to work to put themselves through college and practise all sorts of petty economies——'

'But your mother is absolutely delightful, Verity,' Brad objected. 'Cultured and——'

'She may be, but she's also been a widow for nearly twenty years, she brought up three children single-handedly and my father before he died was only a lowly primary-school teacher. At a state school. Funnily enough,' she paused, 'I didn't think it made any difference either until I met Barry. But now I see it every day. I see it in your old school tie, I see it in the people you know and associate with, I've sent flowers to your mother, so I know she lives in Ascot—so is the Carpenter family mansion, for that matter—and we all can't help knowing that your brother William, for reasons best known to himself, committed the social solecism of marrying outside the clique, which is a bit of a trial, even for as determined a woman as your beloved sister-in-law. And you yourself only a few moments ago alluded to *those* Woods—need I say any more?'

For a moment Brad looked faintly stunned, and it was Sonia who broke the impasse.

She said with a chuckle, 'Ouch! Well said, my dear. But I do feel I can add something here. We aren't all the raving snobs you take us for. And,' she sobered, 'there were other factors to be taken into account regarding Barry's parents. He was their only child, conceived after years of trying—so yes, I have to concede they were blind to a lot of his faults and they probably put enormous pressure on him to succeed, although I *hadn't* realised he was such a drinker. His father has also built up this impressive empire and, in the manner of most fathers, probably counts its ultimate worth in its family continuity.' She stopped, then looked at Verity. 'It's quite possible that your little girl could be a very rich little girl one day.'

'I don't have any ambition for Maddy in that regard.'

Sonia picked up her knife and fork, but then she looked across at Verity and held her gaze for a long moment. 'I see,' she said finally. 'Well. Brad, dear, shall we talk business?'

'Are you—seething with anger?' Brad said as they walked back to the office.

'No. Should I be?'

'Sonia can be a very reserved person, but she did express a desire to see Maddy.'

'She expressed an unspoken desire to reserve judgement,' Verity said coolly.

'I don't think she would go along with anything unjust,' he replied judicially.

Verity walked in silence for a time. Then she said, 'It doesn't matter to me one way or another.'

He stopped walking—they'd arrived at the office anyway—and said, staring down into her eyes, 'Did you love him, Verity?'

'Look,' she answered quite calmly, 'I apologise for airing all my dirty linen at your business lunch, but it doesn't give you the right to harass me for any further details. And would you mind if we got back to work? We have an appointment with the copy-editor in—exactly five minutes.'

'All right,' he returned obligingly. 'Perhaps now is not the time nor place. Like the cockatoo, I'll put that one on hold—I take it you are coming to Port Douglas, by the way?'

Verity took an exasperated breath. 'If I had any sense I'd run a mile,' she said crossly.

He stood back and smiled a shade maliciously. 'No one's stopping you.'

CHAPTER FOUR

THE *Queenslander* pulled out of Roma Street Station at ten past nine on the dot, not three, but four days later, which had given Verity the chance to spend the previous day with Maddy, but, apart from that, little chance to relax over the preceding days at all. In fact, she'd worked late every evening as the ideas she herself had activated had rolled off her boss's brain in a seething mass.

She grimaced as she sank down on to the comfortable seat of her double sleeper and watched the Brisbane suburbs roll by gently. There was no doubt that Brad had come up with three more hilarious scenarios for Len Pearson's Kneg, and there was equally no doubt that Len Pearson was absolutely delighted with the whole concept and was flying up to Port Douglas himself—a town not only dear to his heart because of his charter-boat fleet but also because he grew up there, and to have it as the background for his inventive genius was, to quote him, really tickling him pink. It was not only tickling him pink, Verity mused wryly, it was also loosening his purse-strings quite amazingly, for they were having to fly just about everything, including one bearded Scot, the real McCoy, into the little town for the making of the ads. Not that it was such a little town either any more, he'd assured Verity with palpable pride. With the opening of the Cairns International Airport only seventy miles away and the Port Douglas

Sheraton Mirage, together with its beautiful four-mile beach, its proximity to the Great Barrier Reef and the World-Heritage-listed Daintree Forest, it attracted tourists from all over the world yet still managed to retain its small-town charm.

'I wonder,' she murmured, and turned her head as her door clicked open.

'Wonder?' Brad Morris said, coming in and cocking an eyebrow at her. He'd reverted ever since the day they'd had lunch with Sonia Mallory to his casual attire.

'Nothing,' she said, and yawned.

He grinned. 'Know how you feel. Ever been on one of these before?'

'No. Only suburban trains.' It amazed her slightly that she suddenly didn't even have the energy to feel the usual wariness and annoyance with which she'd viewed this trip from the time it had been mooted, but the fact of the matter was that all she wanted to do was curl upon this comfortable seat and sleep like a log.

'Then I can demonstrate a few things to you. Take this notice, for example,' he said sternly and tapped it. 'Only the conductor can release the upper berth, and no one should be in the lower one when it's being done.'

'I can read, and I have no need of the upper berth.'

'All the same, don't even be tempted. Now here,' he tapped a panel and released it, 'is your wash-basin, your vanity mirror, et cetera, you can hang a few things up in here,' he opened and closed two doors, 'very few,' he added whimsically, 'and right beneath where you're sitting is a portable table that you pull out and stand up in this groove, so. There are two footstools, as you see, pillows up there, and, for complete privacy on the corridor side, this blind that you pull down. What else? Ah,' he turned in the small space, 'facilities. There's a shower in each carriage up that end and toilets at either end, Ladies' down that-away. We are about four cars away from the club car and the dining car, and morning tea will be served soon. And I am right next door, should you require any information about locomotives; it's an electric one at this stage, but we change to diesel at Rockhampton—— I don't think I've ever made you laugh before, Verity!'

Why she should find herself giggling like a schoolgirl was not altogether clear to Verity herself, but she couldn't deny that she was. 'I think,' she attempted to explain, 'it's because I've just realised you're something of a train buff, which is the last thing I would have thought. And something of a little boy about them, too.'

He sat down and stretched out his long legs. 'It never ceases to amaze me, the curious things you believe of me, but yes, I do love trains, they—relax me. It was also an ambition of mine once to be an engine driver.'

'I see what you mean about being relaxing,' she murmured, turning her head to the window. 'I don't know how I'm going to keep my eyes open.'

'Come and have tea first—then I'll leave you alone until lunch.'

He was as good as his word, and after tea she watched the lush, hilly countryside of the Sunshine Coast hinterland pass by with its variety of flowering subtropical trees, banana and pineapple plantations, and those unusual formations known as the Glasshouse

Mountains. She even managed to stay awake until lunchtime and couldn't help being most favourably impressed by the *Queenslander*'s cuisine. She had a seafood platter for lunch that was fresh and excellent and most artistically served. But it and a glass of wine took their toll, and, as the landscape gradually changed to the more common Australian variety of grass and gum-trees, back in her cabin she stretched out and fell dreamlessly asleep.

It was five o'clock when Brad woke her, knocking on her door. She sat up, looked around dazedly then let him in, still flushed from sleep and still looking dazed. He grinned and set the tray he was carrying down on the table.

'Lie back again,' he advised. 'It doesn't do to wake up too quickly. I've brought us a sundowner.'

She grimaced down at her crumpled jeans and ran a hand through her hair, and subsided obediently, although not full-length, and not because she was being obedient. 'I feel awful!'

'One usually does after sleeping during the day on top of a big meal. Unfortunately you can't run it off because we don't stop anywhere long enough until after dinner, but this is the next best thing.' He handed her a glass and sat down himself.

'What is it?'

'Vodka and lime basically. It's my own concoction, a guaranteed pick-me-up that I've perfected over the years. Cheers!'

Verity stared at the tall frosted glass suspiciously, then thought, What the hell? and sipped it. It tasted delicious. She took another sip and sat up.

'See what I mean?'

She had to laugh. 'Can you also guarantee that it won't have me falling flat on my face?'

'Not if you take it slowly. What will complete the cure is a shower and a change before dinner.'

Verity groaned.

'Now, that we *will* be able to walk off, as I mentioned. We stop at Rockhampton for twenty-five minutes. Do you know what they used to call Rocky?'

'No. Tell me,' Verity invited.

He looked at her with a wicked little glint. 'A city of sin, sweat and sorrow. I believe it's improved over the years.'

'I'm glad to hear it.'

They were silent for a time, sipping their drinks idly and watching the sunset cast its pink glow over the landscape while the wheels clicked rhythmically over the rails, until Verity said, unthinkingly, 'This was a better idea than I would have believed.'

He turned his head and studied her comprehensively, with a different glint in his eyes this time. 'Most of my ideas are.'

She tried to regroup her thoughts as she felt her skin prickle beneath that grey gaze. 'I meant, I could become a fan of train travel. That's all.'

'What did you think I meant?'

She swallowed some vodka and lime. Then she sighed and laid her head back. 'I thought you might have meant . . . something along the hoary old lines of *you* knowing what's better for me than *I* do. You would be wrong, Brad.'

His lips twisted. 'Would I? I wonder. But anyway,' he shrugged, 'that's a first. Nearly two years to get one use of my name,' he marvelled. 'You really can't accuse me of being a fast worker, Verity.'

'I wish——' She stopped and bit her lip.

'That I wouldn't joke about it? Then I shall desist,' he said gravely.

'I wish you'd *forget* about it. We might even end up friends, that way.'

'I hesitate to mention it, but in this case you brought the subject up, not me, Verity.'

'Boloney,' she muttered. 'You *looked* at me . . .'

He stretched his legs out sideways and made himself even more comfortable. 'That's interesting. I mean, that you can interpret my looks so accurately. Wouldn't you say it indicated a certain similarity of thought processes? As if we are of the same mind about some things?' he added softly but with his eyes alive and dancing with dangerous little sparks.

'My dear Mr...my dear Brad,' she rephrased coolly, 'all it indicates is that most women can recognise when they are being mentally undressed by a man.'

He laughed and raised his glass in a salute to her. 'I was right about these, wasn't I?' he also said. 'It's quite restored you. And, on the subject of mentally undressing you, I have to be perfectly honest, Verity, and admit that it's becoming a bit of a problem.' He paused. 'I suppose if I told you you have the kind of figure that lends itself to that kind of thing you would take instant umbrage and you'd tell me you can't be held responsible for your body but,' he said humorously, 'there is——'

'Don't go on,' Verity interrupted wearily, and added with asperity, 'You and my mother make a good pair!'

He looked genuinely surprised. 'We agree on that subject?'

'On the subject of—men will be men and even *nice* ones should be allowed a pass or two because they can't help themselves,' she said tartly.

He lifted an amazed eyebrow. 'You actually told your mother what happened? She didn't appear to know, though.'

'Of course I didn't tell her,' Verity said impatiently. 'She . . . guessed.'

'After she met me?'

Verity looked at him darkly. 'If you're going to say that she must have concluded you're a nice man, she did. She's also one of those people who believes *most* people are nice, so don't get too carried away about it.'

'I'm suitably demolished,' he murmured.

'And I'm the Queen of England,' Verity replied witheringly.

He rested his head on his hand and studied his drink for a time, until eventually he said idly, 'Of course, that's not the problem.'

'What isn't? I don't know what you're talking about,' she said, but with less asperity, mainly because some curious instinct was prompting her to defuse her emotions—or perhaps it was the vodka, she reflected rather wryly.

'Those wandering impulses even nice men are subject to,' he said thoughtfully, 'as I was about to postulate before you cut me down—verbally this time, which, I suppose, I should be grateful for, although,' he mused, 'you're very handy with your verbs, so I don't know why I should be that grateful, but it probably is less dangerous than having things thrown at one.'

She grimaced, because she'd obviously left her decision to defuse things until too late, and said with what she hoped was a nice touch of boredom, 'I still don't know what you're talking about—not that it matters.'

'Well, it matters to me—it's my reputation that's at stake, after all——'

'I would have thought you'd be content,' she cut in swiftly, completely unable to help herself, 'to rest on my mother's judgement of you. There certainly can be no kinder interpretation that I can think of, even if she's quite wrong!'

'Don't work yourself up, Verity,' he advised. 'Have some more vodka——'

'Look,' she ran a hand through her hair, 'I just don't know why we have to indulge in this adolescent sort of . . . mating talk!'

'Ah,' he said mildly, but his eyes mocked her, 'at least you recognise it for what it is. But, while mating rituals might have become more civilised—I'm not about to club you on the head and drag you by the hair to my cave—the primitive urge can be less susceptible to civilisation, I'm sure. Adolescent?' He smiled at her, a dangerous little movement of his lips. 'Do you mean unspecific? Then I'll try to remedy that—I was trying to make myself clear anyway. You are not the subject of wandering impulses of the nice kind from my point of view, Verity. I want you—I want to take you to bed, to be *perfectly* specific, and I'd be extremely surprised if you didn't want it too. But I must say in my defence that I've seen hundreds of pretty girls with great figures and, beyond doing what your mother is quite right about occasionally, it's a totally different thing from this. In other words, dear Verity, it's the sum total of *you*, not just your stunning body. And, to further establish my bona fides,' he drained his glass and stood up, 'I'm prepared to wait before I make any more real gestures of the—mating kind until you're prepared to confide in me about your traumatic marriage. Finish your drink; I'll put the tray outside the door,' he added.

Verity stared up at him with such a conflict of emotions chasing through her eyes that he laughed softly, removed the two-thirds-empty glass from her fingers and said softly, 'I think I'll have it before you're tempted to throw it.'

'You're...' But she couldn't go on.

He raised an eyebrow and said with tormenting gravity, 'Not nice at all? Perhaps not, but I don't think niceness really enters this arena. No,' he reflected, 'there's a magnificence about it that goes way beyond anything as pallid as niceness. Why don't you ask yourself why you're in such a magnificent rage, after all?' he suggested. 'I suggest we have dinner at six-thirty. So why don't you also use the shower first? I'll be having a cold one, incidentally. Maybe you should too.'

The shower was steel-lined, the water was lovely and hot, and it was quite an experience on a speeding train going around a series of bends. It also proved to be of assistance to Verity in controlling her temper and dealing with the shocking discovery that she would very much like to scream and scratch as well as throw things.

And, on returning to her cabin, she locked herself in securely, pulled all the blinds down and had a serious heart-to-heart chat with herself as she dressed.

But, despite the palliatives she offered herself and all
the insults she offered her boss, she finally sat down
rather forlornly and knew she had to acknowledge at
least one thing: those minutes she'd spent in Brad
Morris's arms, being kissed and kissing in return, had
been—breathtaking...

She lay back with her eyes closed and, for the first
time since it had happened, allowed herself to remember it all. And it was no consolation to find that
the fierce resistance and will-power she'd used to block
it out of her mind, the anger and blame she'd directed
at him—none of those things had the power to dim-
inish the recollection; the way the fine hairs of her
body stood up and her nipples tingled told their own
tale.

She took several deep breaths and got up to pour
herself a glass of water. 'All right. All right,' she
whispered, 'he got you in the end. And, if you're
completely honest, the only way you can block the
effect he has on you is by attacking and being angry
all the time—and even that may be a curious form of
provocation. You wouldn't be here, stuck on a train
with him, miles from anywhere, otherwise. You would
have left him, and no amount of persuasion would
have made you change your mind. So what does it
all mean?'

She sat down again and hugged herself almost pro-
tectively and stared at nothing in particular for a long
time. 'I'll tell you what it means, Verity,' she said to
herself suddenly. 'This has happened to you before.
This kind of sensual betrayal, even just possessing a
body like this. And look where it got you. Into an
abyss of misery you didn't, at times, ever think you'd
be able to climb out of. You'd be mad if you ever

trusted it again. And while we're on the subject,' she added to herself with a bitter little smile, 'after nearly two years of treating me like a—well, the way I wanted to be treated, but all the same, why is Brad Morris suddenly possessed of this . . . urge to take me to bed, let's be *specific*?'

She didn't have to articulate the answer, it was so obvious. All she had to do was call to mind Primrose Carpenter's exquisite features.

Then she shrugged and decided what she needed to do next was formulate a plan of action for the next week, let alone how to deal with being closeted on this train with him. And that provoked a spark of anger, although she refused to allow it to mushroom into anything more. But really, she did think, he always intended to use this train trip for these purposes. How low is that?

In the absence of any knock on her door at six-thirty, she took herself down to the dining car and discovered the object of her scorn already in the club car and looking at his watch.

'Ah. Thought you might be going to skip dinner, Verity,' he murmured, and added with a roving glance over her fresh grey linen trousers and ivory knitted top, 'You look very nice.'

Verity smiled—well, it felt more like baring her teeth, to be truthful—and murmured, 'Flattery will get you nowhere, Brad.'

He raised an eyebrow but merely returned, 'After you. I've been able to secure a table for two. Aren't we lucky the train isn't full this trip? It usually is.'

'Very lucky.'

He grinned.

* * *

But as they sat opposite each other, separated by the white napery, gleaming silver and glass, it was as if Brad Morris had also formulated a new plan. In other words, he set out to be a charming companion, introduced no sexual overtones—it was she who did that unwittingly—into the conversation, and was almost impossible to resist without Verity's resembling a sullen boor. Of course, the attractive stewardesses were also having a hard time resisting him, and their service was little short of inspired.

'Do they know who you are?' Verity queried at one point.

He shook his head. 'I prefer to travel incognito.'

'That seems a bit sneaky,' Verity commented.

'It's actually the other way around—it obviates the possibility of bribery and corruption.'

'Are you travelling under an assumed name, then? I should have thought the whole country would prick up its ears at the mention of Morris in a travel context.'

He laughed. 'I'm not that famous, although I do get recognised from time to time.'

'I see.'

He looked at her interrogatively. 'What does that mean?'

She looked down at her cheese platter then up into his eyes with a faint, wry smile. 'I was just—well, contemplating the nature of certain things.'

'You're going to have to be more specific than that, Verity,' he said amusedly.

'Well, why these girls should be fluttering around you like moths, for example.'

He grimaced. Then he shrugged and smiled a devilish little smile. 'Search me, Verity. Perhaps their antennae have picked up that I know how to treat women? That I like them and respect them and often regard their bodies as works of art. It certainly can't be my looks,' he said virtuously. 'I know I'm no oil-painting.'

'Yes, well, I guess I walked into that one,' Verity conceded, plucking a bloomy red grape and popping it into her mouth.

'You know,' he leant back thoughtfully and twirled his glass, 'anyone would think I was the only man who'd ever undressed you mentally. I mention it only since *you* expressed the desire to discuss the nature of certain things, of course. I had planned to avoid the subject altogether for a time.'

'I've just lost that desire,' Verity said lightly. 'Apologies for . . .' She gestured.

He regarded her with a curiously unsmiling glance for a moment. Then he said, 'Should we have our coffee and a liqueur at the bar? And I thought, after Rockhampton—where you could ring your mother if you wanted to, incidentally—we might . . . do a bit of work?'

Verity held his gaze with a narrowed glance of her own. 'Why not?' she said at last.

Maddy was fine, so was Lucy, and both thrilled to hear from her so far away. And, due to Brad's knowledge of the train-travelling public's habits—he'd made sure they'd got off as soon as the train had stopped and were first at the public phones before the queue formed—they still had twenty minutes to exercise.

'I really need this,' Verity said as they strode briskly down the platform in the cool, late May night air.

'So do I. You're a fast walker, Mrs Wood.'

'I was once a fast runner, at school. Oh, look, you were right! They're changing the engine.'

'I've mentioned this before, but I'm often right. Tell me,' he went on hastily, 'about your childhood.'

She shrugged. 'There's not a lot to tell. My father died when I was four, I have two older sisters, one lives in Hong Kong and one in Perth, which really kept my mother on the trot as the various grandchildren were born, until, well . . .' She tailed off.

'You needed help with Maddy?'

They came to the end of the platform, and Verity turned abruptly. 'Something like that.'

'Where was your mother when you first needed help so desperately and the Woods wouldn't come to the party? Doing the rounds of the other grandchildren?'

'She was in Hong Kong. My sister there was having a very difficult pregnancy, besides hating the place and finding it difficult to come to terms with the fact that her husband would always want to be roaming around the world,' she finished in an end-of-subject tone of voice.

'All right,' he said mildly.

But Verity stopped suddenly and stared at the sad little tableau being enacted on the platform. Two policemen and a policewoman were escorting a passenger off the second-class section of the train, a girl in her late teens or very early twenties, crying helplessly while the policewoman carried what was obviously her baby. 'What are they doing?' she whispered.

Brad sighed. 'She was smoking marijuana. They were afraid she wouldn't be able to look after the baby, let alone herself, so they had to call ahead for assistance.'

'How do you know?'

'I was talking the train manager before dinner.'

Verity closed her eyes and turned away. And, as if it was the most natural thing in the world, he put his arm around her shoulders. 'Does it bring back—memories?'

'It shouldn't. I never resorted to drugs, and who knows what her circumstances are? But—if she's alone and trying to cope...'

'You know how she feels. Do you think I don't feel sad, watching something like that?'

Verity raised her eyes to his, and what she saw and felt was like a blow to her heart. What she saw in his eyes was the weary sombreness of someone who did feel compassion for other human beings, despite their weaknesses. What she felt was the almost over-whelming urge to rest gratefully in his arms and to submit not only to that compassion but also to any-thing else he cared to do to her. She was, she discovered, achingly aware of him again, and she had to wonder how she could ever have pretended to herself that he did not attract her, that his cleverness did not intrigue her, that you couldn't know him without knowing he'd be a superb lover even before you'd felt his hands on your breasts... How it was suddenly so tempting to think that this might be different.

She turned away abruptly and stumbled.

'Verity.' He took her hand and swung her back. 'Tell me.'

'No. I mean, it's nothing,' she said raggedly. 'I think we're about to leave. Let's ... get to work. On second thoughts, I've got more than enough I can do on my own, so—I'll say goodnight.'

He stared down at her, taking in her unusual lack of colour and agitated eyes, and she couldn't tell what he was thinking at all. But finally he released her hand and said, 'Off you go, then. Goodnight.'

She did work very late for two reasons: to take her mind off Brad Morris and to make sure that she slept. But what she couldn't take her mind off was how she was going to cope with the next day. They didn't reach Cairns, the end of the line, until late afternoon, and then they had an hour's drive to Port Douglas. But surely, she thought, once we're there the pressure will ease a bit? At least the *proximity* must.

In fact, the pressure eased the next day, although not the proximity. But her boss, for reasons best known to himself, was in a businesslike mood for most of the day, thereby lulling Verity into a false sense of security. But also causing her to again feel that cold little void, which in turn was the cause of some bitter self-directed mockery.

'I think that just about sums it all up,' she said that afternoon. 'I'm still worried about a couple of things, but they're outside my jurisdiction, I guess.'

'What are you worried about?'

'The weather, for one thing,' she said wryly. 'It's all very well, talking about filming boating segments, or any outdoor segments, for that matter, but the weather is always a hazard. And it's raining in Cairns, at least,' she added.

'How do you know that?'

'I listened to the weather report on the radio.' She indicated the one built into the wall. They were in his cabin, which was surprisingly tidy. Whatever else he wasn't, Brad Morris was obviously an organised traveller, with all his belongings fitted into one small grip.

'What would I do without you?' he murmured. 'But it never pays to worry too much about anything, you know. We will find a way.'

'You mean, I will have to find a way,' she said a shade tartly. 'The last time we were held up by weather, you and the film crew played cards and left me to deal with all the postponements and cancellations and rebookings—I know,' she gestured, 'it's my job, but I was a nervous wreck by the time it was finally done.'

He looked amused. 'You didn't show it.'

She turned her head away and stared out of the window. They were deeply into sugar-cane country by now, so the view was rather monotonous, but just at that moment she felt as if she could watch it all day— at least it was a respite from the turmoil of her emotions. What was to cause her some surprise was the fact that this was not obvious—that her emotions were in turmoil despite certain resolves she'd made overnight.

'What are you thinking, Verity?' he queried after a few minutes.

She schooled her expression and turned back. 'Nothing much.'

'Is that going to be the answer, do you think?'

She licked her lips but refused to be put out by the narrowed, rather autocratic way of old he was looking at her. 'I don't know what you mean.'

His eyes glinted sardonically. 'That you're going to try to—blank yourself off from this. I can't help wondering what tactics you employ—with yourself, I mean—and perhaps I should warn you that such rigidly self-imposed celibacy on someone who is not of a truly celibate nature can have harmful side-effects.'

Her eyes glinted gold but she restrained herself. 'You can make as much fun of me as you like...' She shrugged.

'I was merely offering advice.'

She smiled faintly. 'I wonder how many men over the millenia have offered that particular bit of advice,' she mused. 'But then again you did tell me once you had a penchant for the hackneyed, didn't you?'

'And *you* once, Verity, melted into my arms and kissed me about as deeply as I've ever been kissed, and you moved your body against mine with a kind of yearning, and you gasped with sheer delight when——'

'Stop it!' she commanded, her eyes now a blazing, angry gold. 'I have no idea what makes you think you have the right to torment me like this——'

'Because it is a torment,' he said with soft mockery and suddenly looking quite relaxed. 'For both of us. That's why——'

'All right!' she flashed. 'So I did...I did what I did, but you're also right about something else! Even hardened celibates probably find times when the flesh is weaker than the spirit—that's all that happened to me, and not without considerable pressure, may I remind you, from you. And considerable expertise, I have no doubt,' she said scathingly. 'But the only conclusion to be drawn from that is—I'm not a block of wood.'

'Are you saying I could seduce a block of wood?' he drawled. 'I doubt it——'

'Oh!' Verity ground her teeth and stood up. 'Stop...'

'Stop working you into a rage, Verity?' he said softly and eyed her quizzically.

'Yes.' She bit her lip but couldn't help adding a little helplessly, 'You really—you really *enjoy* it!'

'I sure do. I'd hate to see you going back to the petrified and perfect Mrs Wood!'

'But we can't—I can't go on like this!' she protested angrily. 'It's just not fair——'

'Maybe. It's not necessary either,' he said with a shrug.

She stared at him. 'And I know what your solution is—don't bother to enlighten me, but the answer is no! How many times do I have to say it?'

'I had in mind another solution for this impasse, Verity,' he murmured. 'It's not new, but during the course of last night and this uncomfortable day my feelings that it is the solution have strengthened. I really think you should tell me about your marriage. Confide in me, in other words. Ever done that?' He lifted an eyebrow at her. 'And then,' he continued, 'we might be able to make a rational and mutual decision as to whether there is any hope for the attraction between us, the mutual attraction, my lovely block of wood,' he said precisely and with no small tinge of irony.

CHAPTER FIVE

'THIS is it?' Verity looked around incredulously.

They'd arrived in Port Douglas after being met in Cairns and driven up by a representative of Len Pearson's charter-boat company in a company four-wheel-drive vehicle. This was standard practice, apparently, for clients of the company to be so met and transported, and Len Pearson had insisted that they avail themselves of the facility. It had been too dark to make much of the scenery along the way or Port Douglas itself, but it could be truly said that the room she now stood blinking on the threshold of in the Club Tropical complex was stunning.

Club Tropical was a new hotel in Port Douglas, Len Pearson had explained in the course of one of his lengthy telephone conversations with Verity. And, wonderful as the Sheraton Mirage was, Club Tropical had the advantage of being in the heart of town, of being very comfortable and modern—indeed, quite imaginative, he'd said with a chuckle, I do advise you to stay there, Mrs Wood, I'm sure Mr Morris will love it . . .

'This is the Bali Suite, Mrs Wood,' the manager of Club Tropical said proudly to Verity. 'We've put Mr Morris in the Reef Suite.'

'Mr Morris' was, in fact, leaning against the doorframe, behind the manager, laughing silently as the manager proceeded to draw Verity into the room and demonstrate all the virtues of the Bali Suite. He was

78

still laughing, but only with his eyes, when the manager left them, having been assured that Mr Morris, whose Reef Suite was right next door, didn't need a guided tour of his facilities.

And he straightened and murmured as the door closed, 'Verity, if you could see your face...'

She tightened her lips and turned away from him exasperatedly.

'What's wrong with it?' he queried then. 'I think it's quite wonderful—a marvellous four-poster bed, complete with draperies,' he gestured towards the bed, 'sumptuous couches, rugs and delightful artefacts, discreet lighting, a subtle blending of colours—pinks and brown and cane—fans and screens, your own louvred patio on to the jungle and just about every mod con, including a video and CD-player and a spacious and luxurious bathroom. I don't understand your reservations.'

'Then I'll tell you,' Verity said precisely and unwisely. 'If ever I've seen a setting more geared towards seduction I can't call it to mind, and if that's what *you* had in mind——'

'I had nothing to do with it!' he protested and started to laugh again. '*You* booked it——'

'Only on Len Pearson's advice,' she shot back. 'I had no idea...it was like this.'

'Perhaps that's what *he* had in mind, then,' he drawled. 'I believe he is due to descend on us some time or another. But how come your thoughts are so irrevocably tuned in to seduction, Verity? I mean, I will admit it would be a nice place to seduce someone in, but to be hit on the head by that very thought the moment you laid eyes on the place is—a little curious, wouldn't you believe?'

'Go away,' Verity said through her teeth. 'Go away before I brain you with one of these delightful artefacts. And don't dare show me your face until tomorrow morning because I would be—it would make me quite sick!'

Of course, he didn't go immediately. He strolled up to her instead and took her wrist and said with sudden dispassion, 'For someone with a name like yours, you display a remarkable disregard for the truth, *Verity*. Have a pleasant evening.' And he released her wrist and left leisurely.

Verity stared at the closed door and then did something totally out of character. She threw herself down on the magnificent four-poster bed, clutched the wonderful pillow in the shape of a butterfly, and had a good, old-fashioned cry.

Presently, and not feeling much better, she got up and unpacked her things and had a long soak in the bath that was the size of a spa. Then she ordered herself something to eat, which she only picked at, and finally, and disconsolately, she went to bed.

She woke at dawn, looked through her 'jungle'—in fact, a wide tropical window-box backed by the leafy environment of Club Tropical—and knew that she desperately needed some exercise. She pulled on jeans, trainers and a white sweater and slipped down the cool, tiled corridors and across the water gardens out into the street.

Club Tropical faced a park that was bounded by the port inlet and the sea, and the grass was wet with dew, there were some wonderful, huge old trees and a sense of freshness and serenity that was something of a balm to her troubled soul. There was also not another person in sight as she explored the park and then the main street of what could still be called, she decided, a rather charming small town. A mixture of old and new, and different, she reflected. It was a while before she could pin down the difference; then she realised it was to do with being in far north Queensland, being in the tropics probably, which laid its own stamp of individuality on things. Such as a warmth in the air, despite its being winter, and the knowledge that this warmth could become a tormenting heat in summer; the lush, tropical vegetation and prolific birdlife, the realisation, she was sure, that life would be lived much more slowly up here. This thought caused her to grimace, and as she walked back past the old wooden pub opposite Club Tropical she advised herself to have her wits about her.

She reinforced this advice with a spa and a brisk swim in the hotel pool before breakfast, and she was feeling considerably better when her boss made his appearance in the Bali Suite—she was on the phone and already drawing together the threads of the operation, as she thought of it, when he tried her door, found it unlocked and walked in.

And one look at his expression was enough to tell her that she might need more than her wits about her today—she would probably need all William Morris's virtues of a saint and the discipline of a brigadier-general rolled into one. Good, she thought with a flicker of humour as she turned away wordlessly while he helped himself to a cup of the coffee she'd brewed—Club Tropical provided not only a coffee maker but fresh beans and a grinder—good. I can handle him like this.

Little to know how wrong she could be.

*   *   *

By the evening of the next day she was in no doubt at all, though. Not only had just about everything that could go wrong gone wrong, but Brad's irritability, which had a low threshold at best, had become little short of catastrophic. But not only that... Where before she'd coped with these situations, not exactly blithely but with assurance and competence, now, despite every effort, she too was tense, and no amount of advising herself helped. And, if anything could be worse than all that, she knew why she was so tense. Not because he was irritable and impossible, not because some essential camera equipment had disappeared into the vast maw of the commercial-airline system and one of the camera crew come out in a mysterious rash which proved to be chicken-pox, to name but a few of the disasters that had befallen them, but because of her new and intolerable awareness of Brad Morris as a potential lover.

She couldn't believe what was happening to her. How could she be struck breathless and lose the thread of what she was saying and doing just by catching sight of his hands or watching him stride across a street? Even worse was the discovery that, while he appeared tall and gangly in his clothes, without them, in the swimming-pool, his body, still tanned from his sojourn in the Whitsundays, was finely made and discreetly muscled, with wide shoulders and narrow hips—and a joy to behold, she thought bleakly once as she watched him surface and pull himself out of the pool with the grace and strength of someone superbly fit.

The other goad to her flesh was the way, unless it was absolutely necessary, he ignored her and treated her as if she were a robot, and she couldn't help herself from raging inwardly about it even while she knew it was only a slightly ostentatious display—had she not indicated that that was how she more or less wanted to be treated?

In her later, saner moments she admitted to herself that it all had to come to a head. At the time, however, on that third evening when they got in from an abortive day's shooting, when she was tired and wet, it had started to rain, and she longed for a bath and a chance to sit down, she couldn't imagine what prompted her to bring it to a head; in fact, it all bubbled up and there didn't seem to be a thing she could do about it.

Because as Brad came into the Bali Suite behind her, slammed the door and opened his mouth to say something damning and cutting, she had no doubt, she turned on him like an angry lioness and hissed, 'Don't say a word! If you're going to blame me because anything resembling a boat makes him sea-sick——'

'I am,' he countered curtly. 'Why didn't you check?'

'Because it didn't enter my head!' she all but shouted. 'I checked his bagpipe-playing ability, his Scots accent, I checked that he owned a kilt and all the paraphernalia that goes with it—I even got you a redheaded one with a red beard, since you're so hooked on redheads. The last thing that occurred to me was that a man built like an ox would...go to water like a kitten once you got him in a boat!'

'You can't help seasickness or a fear of the sea, and you're mixing your metaphors,' he said coldly. 'Look, you goofed; why not admit it?'

It was the last straw. 'If that's how you feel, see how you get along without me, then,' she blazed.

There was a moment's silence as they stared at each other, he with his eyes dark and moody, she suddenly looking white and exhausted and unaware that her thin blue blouse was moulded rather revealingly to her figure. Then he moved his shoulders restlessly and said drily, 'That old gauntlet? It's becoming a bit of a paper tiger, isn't it? How many times are you going to hold me up to ransom——?'

'I'm *not*——'

'Oh, yes, you are, my dear. And all because you *can't* cut the last tie and walk away.'

'No,' Verity whispered and put the back of her hand to her mouth.

'Yes,' he insisted. 'Why do you think we're fighting over something that should be quite funny really? I mean, you're right in some respects. He is built like an ox, he has legs like tree stumps and he'd be the last person you'd want to meet in a bad temper on a dark night. So this inordinate fear of the sea and boats is—well, it shouldn't be so hard to see the funny side of it, with all due respect to his feelings.'

'You were the one who just said I'd "goofed"...'

'Because I'm suffering from the same problem, Verity,' he said deliberately. 'The only difference is, I'm not trying to hide behind a façade of pretence and indifference. A façade, moreover, that does your intelligence and integrity no credit. No, don't,' he gestured as she tried to speak, 'don't give me the old platitude about that being a typical male sentiment over the *millenia* or whatever. Surely we're two adults who can be honest with each other if nothing else? Or are you as rigid and restricted in your thinking to really believe that all men are the same? If I was to

generalise about women like that I can just imagine
your scorn.'

She took her hand away. 'You...you have some
pretty rigid theories on truly beautiful women,' she
said huskily.

'Ah, Primrose.' He smiled without humour. 'What
I neglected to tell you is that her earl is twenty-five
years older than she is, she will be his third wife,
neither of the others being deceased and she's the same
age as his eldest daughter—would you, in all honesty,
be uncritical and not question her motives in a situation like that?'

Verity turned away abruptly, buried her face in her
hands briefly, then turned back and said starkly, 'All
right. All right. I'll tell you what it was like, and why
I'm the way I am; then you might *understand* ...'

He started to say something, paused, then said
quietly, 'Have a shower and get changed first. You're
soaked. I'll make us some coffee in the meantime.'

'So are you.'

'Not really. Well,' he grimaced down at himself,
'I'll change my shirt. Go ahead.'

She showered and donned her jeans and the white
jumper she'd worn earlier. Then she stared at herself
in the mirror as she heard him move around, making
the coffee, and saw that the tension was still there in
her eyes and her mouth and that she looked a bit pale
so that the golden red of her hair appeared darker;
and it occurred to her that she had never really confided in anyone, not the sordid details of it all—was
that what he would expect to hear? she wondered.
And would it be good for her? Or would it lead to
other things that only a fool would get involved in?

*   *   *

'So, where to start?' she said brightly, sitting with her bare feet curled beneath her in a corner of one of the couches, a cup of coffee in her hands. He was about as far away as he could be on the opposite couch and he'd changed into a cotton-knit top and brushed his hair. His feet were also bare, and he'd adjusted the lighting so that it was soft and gentle and closed the glass doors leading to the louvred patio, thereby closing out the sound of the rain.

'At the beginning,' he suggested.

'The beginning was quite commonplace,' she said drily. 'Boy meets girl—well,' she conceded, 'Barry was charming, good-looking, and he had an aura of sophistication, although he was only a year older, that intrigued me. I've asked myself many a time whether it was his money that also intrigued me, and I can't deny that it was pleasant to be driven around in a sports car and taken to good restaurants, to actually be able to go to concerts and sporting events, not just watch them on television, even,' she grimaced, 'to be the object of envy among members of my own sex, but he also had a laid-back approach to life that was...' She shrugged. 'Life wasn't easy for us after my father died—I don't mean it was joyless. My mother is the kind of person who can breathe joy even into the sort of genteel poverty we lived in, but we always had to be so careful, so Barry's attitude was actually refreshing.' She broke off and glanced across at Brad. 'That might be hard to understand unless you've worn hand-me-downs, et cetera, et cetera,' she said ruefully.

'Go on,' he responded idly.

She sipped her coffee then put the cup down. 'It didn't seem to be long after we'd met that I ... began to think I was in love with him. But I was very cautious, and for a time he went along with it. Then ... things,' she plaited her fingers, 'began to get out of hand, and it became harder and harder to say no, and that was when I made a tactical error: I told him I didn't believe in love without marriage, and he pointed out the difficulties of a nineteen-year-old and a twenty-year-old getting married against their parents' wishes, and we had a blazing row—several—and he said finally that I was being ridiculous, and I said if he thought that then we'd better not see each other again, so we didn't for about a month ... And I was miserable and I couldn't help wondering if I was being ridiculous, but I was also piqued because he'd never taken me to meet his parents. For some reason I had it in the back of my mind that it would make things more proper if his parents approved of me, that an intimate relationship might be on the cards then, but anyway,' she gestured, 'he came back and said he couldn't live without me, so marriage it would be, and I ... I went out and did it. Without my mother's knowledge too. You must,' she smiled painfully, 'be wondering what kind of an idiot I was.'

He considered. 'I think it's one of our age-old dilemmas. How to protect young people who have all the feelings of adults but not the wisdom from those kind of mistakes. I mean, you obviously had a good Christian upbringing that was at odds with these liberated times.'

'Kind words; thanks,' she murmured.

It was his turn to smile. 'You also, at nineteen and carefree, spirited, possibly,' his lips twisted, 'a bit headstrong, with a stunning figure and legs like ...' he gestured '... would be enough to turn even Barry

Wood's head, despite what he must have known would be his parents' reaction. My dear, you're right, it's a commonplace story because so many of us are just human.'

She laid her head back and sighed. 'But to be *so* blind.'

'You mean about his drinking?'

'Mmm . . . as well as everything else.' She lifted her head and looked at him. 'I must admit, I was a bit amazed at how much they all drank at first, his crowd, but he never seemed to have any trouble holding it and I suppose I put it down—my amazement—to a lack of sophistication—do you know, he started drinking when he was fifteen? No, you wouldn't, of course, but I really didn't have any idea that whenever he was depressed or frustrated he would literally try to drown it all in alcohol.'

There was a long silence. Then Verity sat up and said briskly, 'I suppose the rest is not hard to guess.'

'No. An unplanned pregnancy,' he raised an eyebrow at her and she nodded, 'his parents' reaction, his allowance cut off—that kind of thing?' Again she nodded. 'I suppose the gradual slide towards him turning violent was only a matter of time. Is that why Maddy doesn't trust men?'

'Yes,' Verity whispered and cleared her throat. 'That was another mistake I made. To let it go on for so long, to ever have let myself live in hope that I could change him. I even threw up college and worked at anything I could get so he could finish his degree and so that what little money he did have we could save towards a home.'

'How long did it go on for? The physical violence?'

'He only attacked me twice; unfortunately, Maddy was old enough the second time to have some understanding of what was going on, and fortunately I had the sense then to just . . . leave. But that's not the only kind of violence, is it?' She looked away and shrugged. 'I have to admit there were times when I indulged in forms of mental cruelty.'

'But—was your mother away all that time?' he queried with a frown.

Verity realised her fingers were still plaited and she unwound them slowly. 'No. If there's one thing that's harder to admit than admitting to yourself you've made a dreadful mistake, it's admitting it to a parent, I've decided. I think it's the guilt, so I tried to brazen it out—well, pretend everything was fine.'

'But——'

'No, Brad,' she stood up and looked through the glass doors, 'it's not possible to tell yourself you're entirely blameless of a serious error of judgement if nothing else. You can't blame it all on being nineteen and a bit headstrong or having a mixed-up set of values, not that kind of disaster.'

'And you don't admit that most people make mistakes?' he queried.

She turned slowly and stared at him for a full minute, with her eyes golden and shadowed, before she said evenly, 'Yes, I do. You see, it's because I know what mine were, that I—am determined not to make the same ones again. I'm not, in fact, as you seem to think, tarring all men with the same brush. I'm simply saying—certain things are not to be trusted. They can mislead you; they certainly misled me, anyway.'

'Ah,' he said slowly, 'I think I begin to see the problem. If you mean what I think you mean, about not being able to trust the sensual side of your nature,' he stopped and smiled faintly, 'join the club, Verity!'

She breathed exasperatedly. 'What do you mean?'

'Just that it's a notorious problem most people suffer from to a greater or lesser extent. What,' he looked at her quite seriously suddenly, 'you're discounting altogether, though, is that we make our mistakes and *learn* from them——'

'I've just told you I *have*,' she pointed out.

'No. You've told me that one mistake has caused you to block off all those very natural impulses and lose faith in them entirely—or at least try to block them off.'

'Brad,' she said very quietly, 'believe me, when you find yourself making up wild and implausible stories to explain away a black eye and a split lip not only is your self-esteem at rock bottom but also your faith in just about everything. But be that as it may, I'm not,' she said, paused, and went on with an effort, 'able to deny any more that I'm...affected by you. But the very way it sprang up out of...well, nothing, leads me to make two judgements.' She stopped and her lips moved into the semblance of a smile. 'Firstly, I'm not as immune to my hormones as I thought I was, and secondly, *you're* not as immune to losing Primrose as you might have thought you were. And that's...about all it amounts to.'

He stared at her narrowly. 'In other words, you think I'm on the rebound?'

She shrugged and nodded.

He swore beneath his breath, then said quite audibly with all his old arrogance and with almost tangible mockery, 'What do you propose we do about it, then, since you've set yourself up as such an expert on these matters?'

It stung, that mockery, she discovered, and she replied in kind without really thinking, 'Why don't you find someone else to—rebound upon? As a matter of fact, I could point out at least two girls who would be delighted to help you get over Primrose: the one in Len Pearson's charter-boat office—she's quite young, but obviously willing—and——'

'Fine. And what will you do?' he shot back. '*As* a matter of fact, I've thought of the perfect solution for you, Verity. Ever thought of taking a "toy-boy" lover? Someone who could help you with your hormones but whom *you* could lay down the law to, say, someone about twenty who you could dazzle with your wonderful legs and breasts—like the kid handling Len's boat today, for example. He couldn't take his eyes off you and all he wanted to do was fetch and carry for you all day—yep, I reckon you could handle him, Verity, and a short interlude with him might just be what you——' He stopped only as she went to hit him, and deftly gathered both her wrists in his hands in an unbreakable grip. 'Now, now, Verity,' he drawled, 'you should try to curb these violent impulses——'

'And you should curb your filthy insults,' she spat. 'Let me *go*.'

'In a moment. Why was my insult any less acceptable than yours? I would have thought we were advising each other to do exactly the same thing and you actually got your advice in first, dear Verity.'

She opened her mouth to dispute that anything she'd said could be as insulting as being advised to take a 'toy-boy' lover, but a sudden spark of honesty compelled her to admit that there was something in what he'd said ...

She breathed deeply and tried to veil any acknowledgement of this revelation from her eyes. 'Just let me go,' she said tautly. 'If you think *this*,' her gaze swung to her wrists and back defiantly to his, 'kind of treatment is liable to advance your cause an inch, you haven't listened to a word I've said to you.'

His teeth glinted in a sudden, mocking little smile. 'You're not frightened of me, Verity,' he said softly. 'You know damned well I'm not about to resort to blacking your eyes. You're only afraid of yourself and living and loving and laughing again because you haven't got the guts to say to yourself, "OK, it happened, but that doesn't mean to say I have to spend the rest of my life like a zombie."' He opened his hands and she reacted like lightning.

She hit out at him, but because she lost her balance at the same time it wasn't that hard or accurate, and she would have fallen over if he hadn't grabbed her about the waist.

'So,' he drawled as she went still, 'I touched a nerve, did I? Let's see if I can do it again—I mean, channel all that furious, nervous energy more productively, or where it belongs, if nothing else.'

But Verity had come to her senses. 'Don't make me kiss you again,' she whispered, and hated herself for the pleading note in her voice.

'It's not a question of making you; I'm inviting you to reciprocate, that's all. It seems to be about the only thing left to do.'

'I hate you,' she said despairingly as he nuzzled the top of her head.

'I know,' he murmured, tilting her chin so that she could see the wicked little glint in his eye. 'Hate away. There are times when I'm in two minds about you. It doesn't seem to change this.' He touched his fingers to her mouth. 'Or the feel of you, the taste of you—which is beginning to haunt my waking and sleeping hours, believe me—the longing to slide my hands right up those long legs, to have time to undress you properly, not just mentally. Seeing you swimming is a special torment, incidentally, despite your very proper togs,' he said, and smiled slightly at the tremor that ran through her body. 'Can you imagine just the two of us in some very private pool late at night, swimming naked? And coming back to a bed like this, relaxed and refreshed?' He paused, and there was no amusement in his gaze as her eyes widened; then she fastened her teeth on her bottom lip. 'So, it's all still there and more so now, and it just won't go away, call it what you will. Is there anything you'd like to add?'

'I knew it!' a delighted voice said behind them, and Verity saw Brad's own teeth shut hard as she started convulsively before his hands fell away and he turned.

'Len,' he said flatly. 'Delighted you could come, but you really should knock, mate.'

Len Pearson was not one whit abashed. He advanced his bulky, balding, pink-jowled personage further into the Bali Suite, saying jovially, 'I did knock! Guess you two were too—er—preoccupied to hear me. But this is excellent!' He rubbed his hands together delightedly. 'I guessed the kind of problems you and Verity were having, you see, and I said to myself, I said, "Len, those two need a push in the right direction and I'll be damned if Club Tropical isn't the just the kind of wonderfully romantic place to do it.'' How right was I?' he queried ingeniously but didn't wait for a reply. 'Well, now that you've got that settled, boyo, I'm sure you'll be able to produce some stunning ads for me. I'm not too old to appreciate that when the fillies are proving troublesome it can put you off your work, your sleep and all sorts of things.' And, so saying, he gave Verity a paternal pat on the bottom. Then he added the straw that broke the camel's back. 'Your brother agrees with me, by the way. He said that in his opinion the one way to keep you happy was to keep Verity with you—and keep you happy too, of course,' he added to Verity.

Of course, Brad saw it coming, but he couldn't keep the reluctant amusement out of his eyes and he started to say something, but Verity beat him to it.

'I don't believe you,' she said to Len Pearson with magnificent, entirely unsimulated scorn and grabbed the back of the couch for support as every last little import of his words sunk in and her eyes started to burn that molten gold. 'What am I?' she demanded. 'Some carrot to be dangled in front of an unwilling horse? Some sort of,' her teeth chattered, 'c-concubine set out to tempt a jaded sheikh? Who gives a damn if he's happy? I don't, and I don't care if no one ever buys a Kneg or the Morris Agency goes out of business or all your charter boats sink and your frozen foods defrost at one and the same time. You can't *use* me like this! How *dare* you? As for you,' she turned to Brad, 'you put me in this impossible position. It's because of *you* that people are talking about me and . . . and . . . using me—I could kill you for that——'

'Verity,' he said grimly, 'where's your sense of humour? Gone west with all your other——?'

'Er—sorry to intrude,' yet another voice said, 'but the door was open.' They all swung round, and it was Bob, who was in charge of the filming operation. 'The thing is,' he continued, 'Hamish, our very own Scot, is in the process of putting together a blinder across the road.' He jerked a thumb in the direction of the pub. 'From the odd things he's said, I gather he's rather mortified about the number of times he threw up today. Especially in front of you, Mrs Wood. A bonny, bonny lass, he—er—called you, strong and shapely and a credit to some place called Lothian, if I've got it right. He believes your ancestors must have come from there anyway. And he seems also to think,' Bob paused and looked embarrassed, 'that you don't treat Mrs Wood properly, Brad. That you were *verry*,' he rolled his 'r's mightily, 'rude to her today.'

There was an incredulous silence. Then Brad drawled, 'You might have been right, Verity. For everyone's peace of mind, we'd have been better to leave you at home.'

CHAPTER SIX

'Mrs Wood—or may I call you Verity?'

'You can call me what you like, Mr Pearson.' It was the next morning, it was pouring, and Verity had just finished breakfast. She had no idea what had transpired with Hamish the night before and she had been just about to pick up the phone to organise transport for herself to Cairns, where she fully intended to catch a flight back to Brisbane.

'I would love a cup of coffee,' Len Pearson said, and sat down in the Bali Suite with every evidence of good humour as well as of being a man with a mission.

Verity sighed, then rose and poured him a cup.

'I came to apologise,' he said earnestly as she handed it to him.

'You don't need to.'

'I most certainly do. To make you feel like a carrot or a concubine was unforgivable!'

Verity winced inwardly—it was impossible not to see, although grimly, the humorous side of it when put like that. She shrugged. 'I probably over-reacted there, Mr Pearson. All the same——'

He sat forward. 'I've had an idea. It occurred to me that you all could do with a day off and that's what I'm going to give you. My yacht is moored in the marina, my crew is standing by——'

'A day off?' she said incredulously. 'Out on the water? Forgive me, Mr Pearson, but that would be like a day in purgatory. It's also raining, in case you hadn't noticed.'

'It will stop.'

Her eyes widened. 'I beg your pardon?'

He waved a large hand. 'I didn't grow up in this part of the world for nothing, Verity, and anyway, I contacted the lighthouse-keeper on the Low Isles and it's lovely out there. It would take us about an hour to get there and then we could have a picnic lunch on the beach, swim, snorkel—you name it, we could do it. I've even persuaded Hamish.'

'Hamish!' Verity raised her eyes heavenwards.

'Uh-huh. You see, it so happens that my mother was a MacDonald from Lothian—Edinburgh, to be precise—and we had a long chat last night about, well, all the things dear to Hamish's heart. What's more, he's now of a much *stouter* heart to do with all things maritime, and if we keep him busy enough and out in the fresh air enough I'm sure we can overcome his *mal de mer*. We might even, although it's ostensibly a holiday, get everyone relaxed enough to do a little shooting.'

'But he's bound to have a hangover—Hamish, I mean—and then there's——' She stopped a bit helplessly.

'Och, as they say back in the Lothians, Verity,' Len Pearson smiled widely, 'he has a very hard head, our Hamish, and I got to him before he did too much damage to it. He also is unaware that *you* might be aware of his sentiments, I've explained that Brad is a little temperamental, and I've sworn Bob to secrecy.'

Verity stared at him. 'You amaze me, Mr Pearson,' she murmured. 'And all in the cause of a Kneg.' She shook her head bewilderedly.

He brightened. 'I'm like that, Verity. It's how I've come to make so much money. Once I get an idea, I just can't let it go. I'm also,' he sighed and looked downcast for a moment again, 'a fairly new widower with no children, so I like to keep busy and *involved*. Will you come?'

'No——'

'Please.'

Verity got up and paced around. 'You might,' she said after a moment, 'have solved Hamish's *mal de mer* but the aversion I'm suffering from towards *Mr* Morris is another matter, and——'

'Ah! Well, Verity,' he broke in genially, 'I've had a bit of a rethink there and I've come to the conclusion that you're right. If there's *anything* you object to in Brad's—er—well, his approach or whatever, if you can see no future for any kind of personal—um—relationship with him, then stick to your guns!'

Surprise caused Verity to pause mid-stride. Len Pearson rose and added, 'I've already seen him, by the way, and told him that he may be a genius in the advertising world, but to force his attentions on any woman is not really the done thing and I'm not too happy about having my Kneg or my frozen foods associated with that kind of behaviour.'

After what seemed like an age Verity closed her mouth, then said, 'You're joking!'

Len Pearson merely looked curiously wise.

'What did he say?'

'Well, it was touch and go for a moment, I suspect, but in the end all he said was something rather strange. He said I should meet your mother.'

Verity blinked.

'Will you come, please, Verity? You see,' he hesitated, 'I used to drive my wife mad with all my inventions, but when I perfected the Kneg, which was just before she died, she said to me, "Len, I think you might have come up with something worthwhile at last."'

The Marina Mirage at Port Douglas was its usual colourful self, despite the rain, which was undoubtedly easing, but Verity couldn't help thinking she would rather have spent the morning browsing through some of the wonderful shops and having an early lunch at the waterside restaurant that overlooked the marina itself and all the boats moored there. Or doing anything but once again being closeted with Brad Morris, even on such a splendid yacht as Len Pearson's *Jessica*. But Len was so proud as he personally gave her a guided tour of its teak, brass and velvet below-decks magnificence, and so happy to have come up with his idea of a 'holiday', even if it was a busman's one, that she couldn't help feeling touched and as if she should make the best of things.

She had no conversation with her boss as they all arranged themselves comfortably up top beneath an awning for the trip, and Hamish, not wearing his kilt but with it in a bag and stowed with the camera equipment, actually joked about getting his sea legs, and quaffed the 'wee dram' Len had had the foresight to offer him as the *Jessica* slid gracefully out of the marina and up the inlet towards the open sea. She'd been unable, however, to stop herself from directing Brad one searching glance to try to divine the nature of his mood. But, if he viewed the day as anything other than a happy diversion, he was not showing it, she decided.

And in the hour—during which the sun broke through and there was just enough breeze to put up the sails—it took them to get to the Low Isles he only addressed one comment to her that would not have been for public consumption. Otherwise he included her quite naturally as he literally held court, and she witnessed Brad Morris, for reasons best known to himself, displaying the magnetic, charming side of his nature so that even Hamish appeared to be won over.

And his one private comment hadn't been all that trenchant, considering what he was capable of. He'd surveyed her as she sat bare-legged on the deck, wearing white shorts and a navy and white spotted blouse with her face raised to the sun and her hair glinting red-gold, and said, 'I've been told you're off-limits today, Mrs Wood. I wonder if he warned everyone else off too?'

She'd simply closed her eyes and examined the sunshot shadows behind her eyelids.

They did everything Len had said they could—swam and snorkelled and explored the small island with its lighthouse and coral reef, with its amazing variety of tropical fish, and then had a wonderful picnic lunch and lazed on the beach for a while.

It was while they were doing this that Hamish stood up suddenly and announced that if he didn't get it right today he never would.

A concerted groan went up, but Brad cocked an eyebrow at Len. 'It's not quite what we had in mind— I mean, its not one of your charter boats with your insignia plastered all over it—but if we could use the *Jessica*, which is much more solid, from Hamish's point of view, to be standing upon, playing the bag-pipes in a breeze——'

'You got it, boyo,' Len said joyfully.

'Now, Hamish, all you have to do is stop playing your bagpipes, look down with obvious distress at your kilt, which, if you stand this way, should blow up like so—don't worry, we won't show the world your under-pants—and Pete here——' Pete was a regular tele-vision performer and he was dressed as a fisherman, complete with rod '—will hand you a Kneg and say, "Get up in a bit of a hurry this morning did you, mate?" Then you give him a withering look but take it, look at it with a frown then flick it open and clamp your kilt up with it just as it starts to blow open again. Now that's all quite simple. The important bit comes next: look relieved, then scratch your beard and say, still looking down at it, "What the devil is it?" in your best Scots accent. Got that?'

Hamish nodded with dignity.

'Good.' Brad turned to Pete.

But Pete pre-empted him with a laugh. 'Then I say in broad Aussie and with a shrug, "No idea, Jock. Thing that puzzles me is what you're doing on this flaming boat anyway." And turn away disgustedly as Hamish goes back to his bagpipes.'

It won't work, Verity thought. To get the timing right, to convey the latent comedy of a fisherman and a kilted Scot playing his bagpipes and stuck on a boat together for no apparent reason with only the sketchy kind of rehearsals we've had so far—it won't work, the wind will die...

But it did. In fact, it worked so well that everyone broke up into helpless laughter as the last skirl of the bagpipes faded away and Hamish, still looking dignified, stared across the boat out to sea.

'Brilliant, Hamish,' Brad called. 'You've done it! You too, Pete.'

Len offered Verity, as the only woman on board, the exclusive use of the main state-room, which had its own shower, to get changed and 'freshen up' if she wanted to. Verity accepted the offer gratefully and closed herself into the luxurious cabin all done out in pink and gold and even boasting a double bed. She had a shower and changed back into her clothes, then as sounds of revelry filtered through she discovered she only felt tired and depressed, lonely and filled with visions of a long, lonely life, visions she'd never before allowed herself to contemplate, and of course with Maddy around it was always easier to batten down on them, but now... She sighed, slipped off her shoes again and lay down on the bed. Just for a few minutes, she told herself, but she fell asleep almost straight away.

It was Brad who woke her. She opened her eyes sleepily and he was standing there with two glasses of what she recognised as vodka and lime. But for a moment they simply stared at each other before he put the glasses down beside the bed and pulled up a stool.

Then he said, 'We thought this might have happened.'

Verity slipped her hand beneath her cheek and glanced at her watch. 'Did you? We must be nearly there.'

He shook his head. 'Everyone was enjoying themselves so much that we took a bit of a detour. We won't be back for another hour. You're missing out on quite an experience.'

She said nothing but propped herself up on her elbow and took a sip of her drink.

The silence lengthened, then he said, 'Funnily enough, I'm not in the mood for,' he gestured upwards, 'all those fun and games any more.'

'I know,' Verity said involuntarily.

He raised an eyebrow and she took an unsteady breath because she could tell from the lines and angles of his face the vague sense of let-down he generally felt after the euphoria of a successful shoot. 'What do you know?' he queried sombrely.

'How you feel.'

'I thought it went well.'

'It did. Despite my reservations, it went wonderfully well.'

He smiled at last. 'Didn't you think I could do it?'

'Not that.' She sipped again then shrugged. 'I'm not in a very positive frame of mind, probably. No, I meant that you always feel a bit let down afterwards, not immediately, but——'

'An hour or so later,' he said with some self-directed mockery. 'How well you know me. And what a cross I must be to live with.'

To her horror, Verity suddenly discovered she had tears on her lashes. She sat up impatiently, dashed at her eyes and took refuge in her vodka and lime, saying after a serious swallow, 'I'd better not take any more afternoon sleeps—I could get addicted to these pick-me-ups.'

'Verity,' he said very quietly and took the glass from her suddenly nerveless fingers, 'why are you crying?'

'I'm not—— I don't know.' She licked her lips despairingly.

'Could it be because this is one of those moments when, irrespective of all the whys and wherefores and dos and don'ts, there might just as well be only you and me on this planet—we can't stay away from each other; we can't even tear our thoughts away?'

She looked at him and couldn't deny it, and it was a long, silent look and she couldn't even tear her eyes away.

He reached out a hand at last and curved it round her cheek and brushed a tear away with his thumb, and it was such an unexpectedly tender gesture that she was lost, quite lost. So that when his lips met hers there was no resistance. And after a deep, searching kiss when his hands moved on her body she felt that wonderful sense of languour that came before the need to give, but she hesitated and hid her face in his shoulder and he merely stroked her hair for a while. Then she looked up with the words framed to tell him she didn't want go any further—and found she couldn't do it. That the rapture was no longer just warm and languorous but becoming electrifying, and she couldn't control her breathing or her pulse-rate or the way her skin shivered of its own accord. It was as if the very centre of her being was linked at that moment to Brad Morris and there was no way she could sever the connection. And instead of saying no she found she could only stare into his eyes, mesmerised and yearning for the warmth and the tenderness to continue so that that part of her soul that had been so brutalised not only by the trauma of her marriage but also by Barry's parents' rejection might heal a little and take some courage from it.

So it was that, with her skin feeling like warm silk beneath his touch, she moved softly as one by one he discarded her clothes then his own, and they might as well have been on another planet as they made that timeless kind of acquaintance new lovers did. She gloried in the way he stared down at her breasts with an indrawn breath, then cupped them and laid the lightest touch on their sensitive peaks with his fingertips. She loved the feel of his hands under her arms and the feel of his long back and broad shoulders beneath hers.

She was helpless when he laid her on the bed and lay beside her and trailed a path of devastation with his lips down her throat and lower and stroked her thighs and her hips. And she touched in return and moved against him at last and more and more urgently at the stunning, wonderful feel of it. And in an equally wonderful way they needed no words; they seemed to know instinctively what pleased, and, as the tempo altered, it did so for them both. And as a kind of wild abandon started to claim her his strength was her saviour, and, once he had entered her and his own kind of abandon took over, she didn't falter but wrapped her arms and legs around him and met and matched his deep thrusting rhythm until an explosion of pleasure claimed them both.

They came back to earth slowly, still wound together and breathing deeply until he lifted his head at last and stared down into her eyes and she stared back. But that was when she began to comprehend, as his gaze held hers captive, that she had no secrets from him now, he knew her most intimate depths, her very essence as a woman and she'd have no defences left—

and the full realisation of what she'd done began to dawn on her.

Perhaps he saw it in her eyes, because a split-second before she moved convulsively he said, 'Verity, don't——'

But she did. 'Let me go!'

'No. Not like this. There's no need——'

'Yes!' she whispered desperately. 'What have I done?'

'Nothing terrible—something quite wonderful, actually, and——'

But, if her own doubts weren't enough, someone chose that moment to knock on the door and call through that they were nearly there, and the full horror of the situation burst into her mind. Of being caught in what could only be called an indiscreet and indelicate situation, to say the least, and using someone else's bed, someone else's boat... She closed her eyes and broke into a cold sweat as she waited for the door to open, but it didn't and she heard footsteps retreating, although that didn't lessen her anguish a lot as Brad sat up abruptly.

'Bloody hell,' he swore softly. 'I'm beginning to think we're jinxed. Why can't people just leave us alone?'

'If he'd opened the door...' She put her hands to her face, going as hot as she'd been cold.

'He couldn't. I locked it. Do you think I *wanted* an audience?'

She took her hands away. 'When? When did you lock it?'

'When it appeared that what happened was inevitable,' he said evenly. 'I didn't come down here with the express purpose of seducing you, Verity, if that's what you had in mind.'

'Oh!' She sat up and pulled the bed-cover over her. 'All the same, can you imagine the...looks and the speculation going on up there? The ''wonder what they're doing behind locked doors'' kind of comments? I must be mad!'

'No.' He took her wrist and stared into her agitated eyes. 'Marvellous and warmer than I'd thought possible, generous, exquisitely sensual,' he said deliberately, 'but lost and lonely—well, there's no need to be that way any more, and there's no need to give a damn about what anyone else *thinks*.'

But she tore her wrist free. 'And what about what *I* think?' she shot at him.

He sat back. 'Tell me,' he said with a twisted little smile but a glint of something darker in his eyes. 'I've no doubt it will be a revelation.'

For a wild moment Verity contemplated telling him that he was responsible for what had happened, he had seduced her or exercised some strange power over her—but only for a moment, as a stronger voice within her told her to be honest at least. So, what to say? she wondered a little frantically. It can't work for us, you can't be held responsible for the fact that I'm battered and bruised mentally, and *I'm* not interested in an affair and I still believe you're trying to exorcise Primrose anyway? Don't forget, I was the one who not only sent her the flowers and whatnot, but I also knew what you did, how *together* you were for so long, how you looked at her in the office...

She breathed deeply and said merely, not looking at him, 'If you think I'm going to walk off this boat arm in arm with you, you're mistaken.'

'Verity?'

She looked up at last.

'Say that again!' he commanded.

A flood of colour rose up her throat. 'Just go away, Brad,' she whispered.

He smiled slowly, a savage, tigerish smile that didn't hide the contempt in his eyes. 'Do you really have such a small, trite little soul?' he marvelled. 'Is that all you can say after an experience like that? Believe me, I've done my best not to be typically cynical about women.' He paused and reached for his trunks and shorts, then shrugged on his T-shirt. 'But I'm beginning to wonder what does go on in their minds. I shall relieve you of my presence, Verity,' he added, strolling over to the mirror and running his hand carelessly through his hair. 'And I shall go up top and compound the,' he paused again and swung round to look at her with an incisive glance that seemed to cut her to the quick, 'sacrilege by telling everyone we were working on the next riveting chapter of the Kneg saga.'

And he left, closing the door with almost insulting gentleness behind him.

There was a church in the park that skirted the Port Douglas inlet. A little white wooden non-denominational church called St Mary's-by-the-Sea with a long history, although the building had been moved and restored several times after cyclone damage.

What she hoped to gain as she walked up the steps and into its simple interior, Verity wasn't sure. She'd slipped away and decided to walk back to the hotel from the marina and left everyone still carousing on the *Jessica*. Brad had not even looked in her direction as she'd made her excuses to Len. In fact, it had appeared to her that most of them were rather careful not to look at her too closely.

She stood for a while, staring at the stained-glass window depicting someone picking up sea shells, and then out through the open wooden shutters behind the altar that framed a lovely view of the inlet bathed in the golden light of the setting sun. Then she sat down, leant back and closed her eyes and tried to defend herself against certain charges: of smallness and triteness of mind, for example, not to mention committing sacrilege. But the only thing that came to mind was an overpowering sense of melancholy and the feeling that he might have been right. At least, about *her*. She'd given herself with an intensity that made all her earlier, even happy recollections of sex before it had become like a war pale by comparison. And then she'd drawn back from it...

But for him? she wondered. Could it have been such a momentous experience? That he was unlikely to find with any other woman?

She opened her eyes and stared down at her hands and was surprised to see them gripped tightly together—she couldn't remember doing it, although she did understand why she might have done it. Because she was staring one fact in the face at last. She'd done the one thing she'd thought it was impossible for her to do, and she was terrified. Of herself and whether she was once again making a terrible mistake; of him and whether he knew what he was unleashing...

She trembled and tried to resist it, the memory of their lovemaking, but couldn't, so she got up and ran out of the little church and all the way back to Club

Tropical, where she sat down and immediately made her daily phone call to Lucy and Maddy—the only thing she could think of that would restore her to some sort of normality.

CHAPTER SEVEN

'THE Daintree Forest—the Wet Tropics World Heritage Area, in other words,' the guide said proudly, 'contains the oldest surviving rain forests in the world. They've been around for more than a hundred million years!'

Verity stared out of the window of the deluxe four-wheel-drive vehicle at the towering forest on either side of the saturated red ribbon of mud that passed for a road and assimilated some other interesting facts about the Daintree—that sixty per cent of Australia's bat species, sixty-two per cent of the butterflies lived in this point-one per cent of the continent, as well as two species of kangaroos that were very rare and different, kangaroos that climbed trees and moved backwards. There were also crocodiles, as one couldn't fail to be aware of from the moment you drove aboard the ferry that took traffic across the Daintree River and you observed the signs similar to no-smoking signs but with a swimmer and rampant crocodile featured. As for the varieties of plants, the list was endless. And she could believe it all as the dripping, impenetrable-looking foliage passed slowly by. The road was not only waterlogged but very narrow, very steep and winding.

The problem was, she just couldn't raise much enthusiasm for the Daintree; in fact, she found it rather claustrophobic and menacing. Perhaps a dry, sunny day might have helped, she thought with a sigh, but knew in her heart it was not so. And then there was the irony that their destination, Cape Tribulation, so called because Captain Cook happened to be sailing past in 1770 when he ran into the Great Barrier Reef and holed his ship, so aptly echoed her situation in name. Deeply troubled, to put it mildly.

The beach at Cape 'Trib', as the locals fondly called it, had been chosen for the second in the Kneg series, and it made Verity feel incredibly weary just to think of it.

But it too went well, so well that she couldn't help feeling that the Kneg ads were beginning to have a classic feel about them, and it made her smile faintly to think that Len Pearson just might go down in history as an inventor. It also was impossible not to appreciate that Brad had moved into another gear, so to speak. If he'd been inspired with Hamish and the boating sequence, he was even more so on the beautiful sands of Cape Tribulation, where the rain stopped and the sun shone and a thirst-crazed wanderer—a spare member of the camera crew who was an amateur actor in disguise—found a Kneg on the beach and managed to carve a hole in a coconut with it and drink the milk, then stare down at it with acute puzzlement.

On the way back they stopped at the lovely and aptly named Coconut Beach Rain Forest Resort for lunch—they were obviously not going to be allowed to escape any feature of the area, so great was Len's pride in it—but the day was fast approaching a nightmare for Verity and again she was unable to find any real enthusiasm . . . for anything, food included.

So she decided to go for a walk along the beach, and so deep in thought was she that when she came to a creek bed that cut a swath of rippling channels across the beach, and wound behind it was a shallow, dark, tree-lined chasm, she stopped walking and just stood there, staring at nothing in particular, thinking in circles. Bitter little circles around herself and Brad, but with most of the bitterness directed at herself.

But I don't know why I should feel this way, she reflected. I don't really know why I can't get out of my mind his accusation that it was a trite, small-minded way to behave. To even feel guilty...

Something moved up the creek bank, she just caught it out of the corner of her eye, and instantly she was filled with a churning sense of panic and but one thought on her mind—was it a crocodile? And for a frozen moment her legs wouldn't work. Then she spun round and ran straight into Brad.

'Whoa!' he said, fielding her. 'I didn't mean to frighten the life out of you.'

'You didn't!' she gasped. 'I thought—something moved back there. I thought it was a crocodile.'

'I doubt it——'

'Why?' She said frantically, trying to evade his grasp. 'Everywhere you go up here there are warning signs about crocodiles!'

'So there are, but, assuming it was one in the first place, it would have been upon you and attacking you by now, if that's what it had on its mind, and in the second place, while people have undoubtedly been attacked, it's a very uncommon occurrence. It was probably a lizard.'

Verity looked over her shoulder fearfully but there was absolutely nothing to see, which not only made her feel foolish but correspondingly cross. 'It *might* have been a crocodile,' she said witheringly.

He smiled down at her, a mocking little smile. 'A lot of things *might* have been, Verity. The trouble with you is, you see problems where there aren't any, and——'

'Let's not get personal,' she broke in tautly. 'And would you mind letting me go?'

'When I'm ready,' he responded. He had his hands on her waist and he leisurely inspected the cream cotton blouse she wore with khaki knee-length shorts. 'After all,' he said finally as a tinge of pink came to her cheeks, 'we're not exactly strangers, are we?'

'What's that got to do with it?' she countered.

'Well, despite the fact that I find your... ways somewhat strange, I can still appreciate that you got a fright. In fact, I can still feel your heart banging away merrily, although I'm tempted to wonder if it's because of your crocodile now—or me.'

'Don't pride yourself on too much, Brad,' she warned angrily. 'It's not every day I see, even mistakenly, a salt-water, possibly man-eating crocodile——'

'And it's not every day that *I* get made love to so wonderfully and then have the door slammed in my face, so to speak. Almost as if I were a man-eating,' he paused and smiled, not pleasantly, 'make that a *woman*-eating monster. A curious analogy, but, I'm sure you'll agree, in the circumstances, quite appropriate. You really should have stopped me, you know, if you were going to feel like this.'

Verity stared up into his grey eyes, suddenly arrested, because, of course, there lay the root of all her guilt and confusion. She closed her eyes briefly. 'Well, I didn't,' she said tonelessly and then, with more spirit, 'Do you really believe that makes me——? I'm sure there's a name for it——'

'There is,' he agreed, and said no more, but the way his gaze dwelt lazily on her mouth then her breasts beneath the cream cotton was at the same time so intimate and so insolent that Verity felt seared, and also at the same time as if she were back on the *Jessica* with him, lying naked beneath him, revelling in all he did to her.

She took a despairing breath and wrenched herself free, her emotions in such a turmoil that her heart had started to beat in a way no mere crocodile would have induced it to. 'All *right*,' she said through her teeth, 'it was a stupid thing to do. But the stupidity wasn't only on my side. It was actually a crazy thing to do! I know you take a pretty casual view of things, but to allow ourselves to get so carried away, to...to,' she stuttered, 'lay ourselves open to more or less being caught...caught——'

'*In flagrante delicto*?' he drawled. 'We didn't. I told you, I locked the door.'

'And you don't think that was as good as shouting it from the roof-tops?' she said sardonically. 'Have you not noticed how everyone is looking at us—or refraining from looking at us?'

'Verity, we had this out yesterday. I'll grant you, it was unfortunate, but it's not the real issue,' he said grimly.

'Oh, but it is, Brad.' She hesitated, but the words were building up in her and, rightly or wrongly, she couldn't help herself from saying them. 'I've never behaved like that in my life and I just hope to God I'm never tempted to again! I...it's madness, a kind of madness, and I wish you'd just forget it all, let alone...' Something stopped her then, though too late.

'Let alone leading you astray? Is that what you were going to say?'

She bit her lip and had to look away from his cool, suddenly almost clinical gaze.

'What a fraud you are, my dear,' he went on softly but with an inlay of sheer contempt. 'You loved it, you'd love it again and again, wherever and whenever—is that why you're running so scared? Because once you start you're insatiable?'

It was so cruel that every vestige of colour drained from her face, and she swayed slightly. Then she was prompted to cry that she *was* running scared, but of falling desperately and irrevocably in love with him; that was what she feared was being unleashed within her. But finally pride came to her aid. She said huskily, 'Brad, if you honestly believe that, to ever want to have anything to do with me again would be—no better than what you think I am.' And she turned on her heel and walked surprisingly steadily back to the resort. He made no attempt to catch her up.

Back in the Land Rover, she steeled herself to try to act normally, but it was an incredible effort and she had no idea how she was going to cope while they made the rest of the series or whether she should even try...

And she was never more relieved than when she was at last able to close herself into the Bali Suite as darkness claimed far north Queensland. In fact, she sat slumped on one of the couches for an age in the dark before she wearily got up to run a bath.

The phone rang just as she stepped out of it and she was about to ignore it, then thought it might be

Lucy, so she ran over to answer it, wrapped in a towel. It was Brad.

'Verity?'

'Oh ... Yes?'

'Look, I'm having a conference—rather, I'd like to have a conference—but you have most of the paperwork, the art lay-outs and copy, et cetera for the charter-boat literature, so I thought we might as well hold it in the Bali Suite,' he said with unmistakable irony.

'What—now?' she replied incredulously.

'What's wrong with now?' he drawled. 'The sooner we get this wrapped up, the sooner we can all go home.'

'But I'm not even dressed ...' She broke off and bit her lip. 'I haven't eaten,' she added.

'None of us has. I'll order something to be sent up. As for being undressed, did you have anything particular in mind? If so, I hope you've chosen a partner wisely, someone who understands all your little quirks—mightn't it be an idea to send him along to me first? I could tell him what to expect.'

'You can also go to hell, Brad Morris,' she said coldly and with incredible restraint. 'But do stop in on your way,' she added cordially. 'There's nothing I'd like better than to get this ghastly roadshow over and done with, even if it means working night and day.' She slammed the phone down.

It was a mistake, of course. It was like flinging the gauntlet down to a highly superior enemy, one much better versed in the art of warfare—in this case, the subtle art of a war of words—and by the time the conference was over she had, through every other emotion, to marvel at how he'd done it. How he'd contrived without exactly saying so to let everyone know that a state of war existed between them, to make everyone thoroughly uncomfortable and glad to be able to escape, and to make her feel like a limp rag.

In fact, all she could do as they left was retreat to the patio with a tray of coffee-cups, and assume as she heard the door close that he had left too. She stared down at the counter she'd placed the tray on, then turned to the open green louvres and took several deep breaths to compose herself as she caught that familiar feeling creeping in, that lonely, melancholy feeling. And she clenched her fists and wondered bitterly and with a little flicker of anger why she should feel like this about a man who could humiliate and had humiliated her publicly once again, let alone who could say what he'd said to her in private. There could be no doubt in anyone's mind after tonight that something deeply and darkly personal was going on between them. Even if they hadn't caught the implication of his words, the sardonic glint of his eyes every time they'd rested on her had made it all abundantly clear.

He really is a bastard, she thought, and tensed as one by one the lights clicked off behind her. The last to go was the one on the patio, and she swung round incredulously. But it took a moment or two for her eyes to adjust to the relative darkness—there was some faint light coming up from the water gardens below. Then she could distinguish his outline silhouetted in the doorway only feet from her, and gradually more details. He was standing with his hands shoved into his pockets, his shoulders relaxed, but he was watching her steadily.

And as the first shock passed it was replaced by another. Because her first instinct—to retaliate as cuttingly and contemptuously as she knew how—was curiously swamped by something else. It was like a rising tide, she discovered as they stood staring at each other, of singular awareness not only of him but also of herself and everything around them—such as that there was also moonlight filtering through some clouds, and the haunting perfume of a tropical shrub wafting on the faint breeze. It was the feel of all the fine hairs on her body standing up and the divining that she felt restless and unfinished, still angry and not to be placated, but once again as if there were only the two of them in the world. And, to put it even more simply, she reflected, to be in the awful position of being incredibly attracted to a man you often hated.

He broke the silence. He said in a cool, clipped voice, 'Are you feeling the way I am, by any chance, Verity?'

She made no gesture; her pride wouldn't allow her to. 'I'm not sure what you're feeling, Brad. But—and you may accuse me of further pettiness of mind when I say this—things are not so simple between us as you seem to think, and to make the whole world privy to...' She hesitated.

'Our problems?' he supplied drily.

'... our problems,' she agreed with irony, 'is, to my mind, extremely petty, not to mention trite, and the sign of a severely wounded ego, if I may say so.'

'You may,' he responded, 'not that you'd be right.'

She did make a helpless little gesture then, and she turned away.

'Not entirely right—I'll amend that,' he said. 'Yes, my ego was somewhat wounded, since you mention it. To be so—good together and not to be able to repeat the experience is naturally galling, and I suppose it's only human to ask yourself what you might have done wrong. And then human also to go on the defensive and exhibit classic symptoms of a bashed-up ego—perhaps you were about halfway right,' he conceded, and waited until she turned with a reluctant smile playing on her lips before adding, 'I'm glad I've amused you.'

She put a hand on the railing. 'You haven't. Not really.'

'You were smiling.'

She shrugged. 'A momentary weakness.'

'As was the other?' he queried with a lifted eyebrow.

'As was the other,' she agreed, not with defiance and not caring how she would be judged again, but with simple honesty, and she stared down at her hand gripping the railing then lifted her gaze to his, but there wasn't enough light to make out the expression in his eyes. And she tensed as he took a few steps towards her. 'Brad . . .' she said, but her voice got caught in her throat and she found she could only stare helplessly up at him.

But he made no move to touch her, his hands still pushed into his pockets, and at this range she could look into his grey eyes but be unable to decipher them. And he said with little inflexion, 'But that's only half the story, isn't it, Verity? You've made up your mind this is not to be. You've probably cited to yourself a dozen good reasons why it couldn't work, shouldn't be allowed to exist—you're ignoring one basic fact: it *exists*, whether you like it or not. Right now, for example, you're terrified that I'm going to touch you because that would weaken your resistance and allow your senses to speak for you.'

He stopped, then as she stirred restlessly he went on in the same even voice, 'Don't imagine the same isn't happening to me—I'm tired but I know I won't be able to sleep. I'm—fed up and wishing to God I'd never heard of a Kneg let alone been roped in to promote it, but then again if someone dropped the world rights to promote Coca Cola in my lap right now I'd feel the same. Because of you.'

'Brad——'

'Let me finish,' he said quietly. 'Of course, that would be no concern of yours—if you weren't standing so still in the moonlight, if you didn't look tired and strung up, haunted and hauntingly desirable—for the same reason. So, we're in this together. It's that same basic fact.'

She licked her lips but forced herself to speak. 'And do you believe that that one simple fact is going to take care of all the problems between us, Brad?'

'No,' he said sombrely. 'That would be naïve. But to deny it is like killing something before it's had a chance to live, it's like denying hope—and that's a dangerous way to be.'

'Have you any conception of how I might be if I have an affair with you that . . . that ends negatively?' she whispered.

'Why are you so automatically assuming it has to end negatively, Verity? What *is* your definition of a negative affair, by the way? One that doesn't end in wedding bells? I would have thought you'd learnt that lesson the hard way.'

She gasped. 'That's as good as saying it won't!' She stopped abruptly.

'No,' he countered. 'It's saying that a lot more can exist between a man and a woman than an *automatic* progression to the altar. It's saying that, whatever happens between us in the future, right *now* we're inextricably bound together and you're running away from it for no good reason——'

'Are you sure you're not rehearsing good copy in favour of promiscuity?' she broke in mockingly.

He took his hands out of his pockets at last and folded his arms. 'Are you sure you shouldn't be wearing a placard saying "Don't look, don't touch unless you're prepared to tender a marriage licence", Verity?' he drawled.

She was unable to conceal the flash of pain in her eyes, and a spark of confusion.

If he saw it he made no direct comment, but then she knew he must have because he said differently, 'You don't honestly believe I'm *toying* with you, do you?'

She bit her lip.

'Or that this has anything to do with promiscuity?'

'I...' Her shoulders sagged suddenly. 'No. It has to do with not wanting to be hurt again, I guess,' she said huskily and starkly.

'And you think I have a record of going around deliberately hurting women?' He smiled, a brief, chiselled movement of his lips. 'I'm prepared to admit to a lot of faults, but that's a new one to me.'

She blinked several times in an attempt to evade the compelling grey glance, but it was no good. She sighed. 'No. But it doesn't change the fact that,' her voice quickened in a kind of desperation, 'I don't know what to do! I...' But she couldn't go on and she bowed her head and fought back humiliating tears at the same time as she wondered why she hadn't cited the one thing that was her biggest stumbling block, the one person, to be exact—Primrose. Because, she thought, I just know he's not going to admit he's on the rebound—I doubt if he's even admitted it to himself. Or was that an admission of a kind? The bit about all the things that can go on between a man and a woman—such as wanting me but still *loving* her . . .

He watched and waited.

'There are times when I hate you, like this evening.' She looked up tautly but with no more than a suspicious brightness in her eyes.

'I don't think that matters,' he said gravely.

'Of course it must!'

'No. Not when it's the other side of this.' He took the last step and put his hands on her shoulders then let his fingers roam up the slender line of her throat.

She couldn't help herself. She tilted her head back and shivered with pleasure, and when he looked into her eyes it was to see the mute acknowledgement that her senses were trapped before she closed them wearily.

'Don't look like that,' he said barely audibly and touched her lips with one finger.

'I must. And I'll probably want to fight you again,' she whispered raggedly. 'Don't imagine——'

'I won't,' he promised but stifled any further speech by the simple expedient of kissing her.

'I think you should go.'

He stirred beside her. They were covered only by a sheet, and the Bali Suite was in darkness. 'To protect my reputation or yours?'

'Ours,' she said. 'Besides which, I'm plagued by memories of people knocking on doors.'

He linked his fingers through hers. 'I know what you mean. But it's far too late—or early—for that.'

'Don't you believe it,' she said ruefully.

'I hope you don't always associate that—with this.'

'So do I.' She bit her lip.

'Was it any good?' He let go of her hand, propped himself on an elbow and reached out to switch on a lamp.

Verity blinked several times and drew the sheet up further, causing an absent smile to flicker across his lips, but he didn't attempt to disrupt it. 'Isn't that akin to asking—was I any good?' she said barely audibly.

He looked wry. 'All right. Was I?'

'I meant,' she hesitated, cursing herself, 'I don't think we need to indulge in post-mortems.'

'You may not,' he replied, 'but don't forget my bashed-up ego. It would be kinder to tell me.'

She sighed, then had to smile reluctantly. 'You were fine and it was . . .' But she broke off and turned away abruptly to lie on her back as patches of heat started to steal up her throat. 'Don't make me do this,' she said huskily. 'It's quite juvenile.'

'I have to disagree—you certainly couldn't call what we did juvenile, therefore any discussion of it shouldn't be juvenile—perhaps humorous, if you'd let it be—but not to say anything at all,' he murmured and tucked the sheet in around her solicitously and in a way that made her feel foolish, 'is rather denigrating it, wouldn't you agree?'

'No, obviously I don't,' she responded with an effort. 'Anyway, it must have *been* obvious what I thought of it.'

'You're not ashamed of being wild and wonderful, are you, Verity? What I said earlier today was the words of a deeply frustrated male person and——'

'I'm not.' But she sat up jerkily again and it wasn't quite clear to her whether she was ashamed and denying it or calling a halt to any further discussion on the subject. Probably a bit of both, she thought gloomily. 'Look,' she said rather drily, 'it was...wonderful, as you very well know, and you were...the same, but I reserve the right to...to... Oh!' She turned to look at him exasperatedly.

'Keep your thoughts to yourself?' he said lazily.

'Yes. I did warn you.'

'So you did,' he said softly and drew his fingers idly down her spine.

She trembled in spite of herself, and had to make herself go on. 'I also reserve the right not to have you getting caught leaving my room at a questionable time and in compromising circumstances—and please don't start on about sacrilege again,' she warned, 'because I don't care what it makes me or how small and trite but I prefer to be very private about these things. I also have to work with you tomorrow. We have an early start, moreover, and, if that's not bad enough, we have to hike up Mossman Gorge and perform miracles with a Kneg on a suspension bridge over the raging Mossman River—— Don't do that,' she said in quite a different voice.

He laughed softly and took his fingers from her spine. 'What am I allowed to do?'

'Just go,' she said with an effort. And added in a voice that quavered ridiculously, 'P-please.'

'OK. I'll consider myself banished, Verity. Well, when I've done this...' Which was to kiss her lingeringly then tuck her up again. 'But I'll be back.' He pushed the red-gold strands of her fringe off her forehead and stared down at her with a sort of quizzical amusement, and added, 'It's just as well I'm not really possessed of a wounded ego, isn't it? I could go out and shoot myself—had you thought of that?'

'I never for one moment believed you were.' But she couldn't stop herself from answering that amusement in his eyes with a faint curve of her lips. She sobered almost immediately, though. 'Brad, tomorrow...?'

'What the hell do you imagine I'm going to do?' He sat back with his old look of impatience and she flinched.

'It's going to be difficult enough to do this as it is,' she said stubbornly, however. 'And I do have to get back to Maddy.'

He narrowed his eyes then said quietly, 'She means an awful lot to you, doesn't she?'

'The world,' Verity answered simply.

He said, after a few moments, 'She's a lucky kid.' And left not long afterwards.

But it was a while before Verity got to sleep; she found herself hugging the spare pillow and staring into the darkness for an age as she tried to contemplate the future.

CHAPTER EIGHT

'ANOTHER good day's shooting,' Len Pearson said excitedly. 'If these ads don't sell my Kneg, I'll eat my hat.' And, 'Only one to go, boyo!' as he slapped Brad heartily on the back. 'I know you were dubious about doing the whole caboodle up here, but it's worked a treat.' His face fell. 'If only my Jess had lived to see them. She grew up in Port Douglas too, you know. She loved it.'

'As a matter of fact, I've thought of putting something into the last one that clearly shows it is Port Douglas,' Brad said rather gently.

Len brightened, and they got into an earnest discussion on what was the best way to do it.

Verity watched them for a moment then turned away with her heart beating erratically. It was not yet twenty-four hours since they'd slept together for the second time, and, although it was she who had insisted they give no intimation to anyone that they had, it was she who had had difficulty concentrating all day. And not so much, curiously, because of the serious misgivings that were lying just below the surface of her mind, but because of the visions that had plagued her all day: of lying in his arms, mute but consumed by desire, memories of the things she'd done, although she'd kept such strict control on what she'd said, thoughts of the night that lay ahead ...

She closed her eyes and took herself to task and was consequently brisker than absolutely necessary as she made her excuses—they were all having a sun-downer in the pub across the road to celebrate the successful shoot.

'Stay a while, Verity,' Len pleaded.

'I can't,' she said but softened it with a smile. 'We left too early for me to ring Maddy this morning, so she'll be waiting for a call.'

'Oh, well, I guess we should let you go—what do you say, Brad?'

'By all means.'

To her dismay, Verity found herself hesitating, but he said no more and turned to Bob.

She left, but as she crossed the road she found herself wondering what 'by all means' actually meant. That he would come? That he wouldn't because he found the secrecy she'd insisted on ridiculous? He'd gone along with it all day, however, although there'd been times when she'd discerned a devilish little glint in his eyes—damn, she thought. *This* is ridiculous.

She had a long chat with Maddy and Lucy, and they were both delighted with the postcards they'd received, and Lucy let slip that her sister Helen was getting about more and more.

'It should only be another couple of days at the most, Mum,' Verity said. 'Is Maddy——?'

'Maddy's fine, darling. Missing you, of course, but there's so much here for her to do. I must warn you that she's adopted a kitten!'

'I expected no less,' Verity said with a laugh. 'Not that I'm crazy about cats, but it could have been a lamb or a duck.'

'And how is it going up there? Are you coping with Mr Morris?'

For a split-second Verity was plagued by an image of herself and Mr Morris entwined on the four-poster bed, and she had to swallow hard before she said, normally, she hoped, 'Yes. He hasn't been too bad. Um... apart from the odd day.' And closed her eyes and felt herself break out into a sweat that was to do with lying by evasion as well as a lot of other things.

But it was when she put the phone down at last that everything that had been lying just below the surface of her mind all day rose up to torment her. How to tell her mother, for example. How to go on working for him in less rarefied circumstances than these. And it was over an hour before he came. During which she showered and washed her hair and blow-dried it, and changed into a pair of oyster trousers and a long-sleeved, silky cinnamon blouse, tucked in and belted round the waist by a leather belt with an intricate brass buckle. She even put on some make-up. But as she stared at herself in the mirror and decided she looked groomed, slim but taut, she had also to ask herself what she thought she was doing. Making a statement of some kind? Trying to deny that all day all her senses had been homed in on this time, when he'd come to her or with her and take her in his arms and...

She shook herself slightly and tried another tack— You're on the right track, kid, she told herself with totally false humour. You might have laid down some arms, but you don't have to lie down and beg—— Oh, *hell*, is that why I'm feeling all churned up? Because he hasn't dropped everything and come...? If that's so, you better change your tune.

But that, although she didn't know it, was to prove unexpectedly difficult.

He came not long afterwards, neither changed nor showered, and it was not hard to guess that he'd come straight from the pub.

'You didn't have to,' she said coolly and winced inwardly as she let him in and led the way.

'Didn't have to what?' he queried.

'Tear yourself away,' she said over her shoulder before she could stop herself, and gritted her teeth and sat down on a couch.

'It was the opposite, actually,' he replied, coming to stand directly in front of her and flexing his shoulders as if he'd been sitting too long. 'I, speaking figuratively, had to bolt myself down. Otherwise I would have got up and run after you across the road like a lovesick teenager. Which I didn't think you would appreciate.'

'I wouldn't——'

'On the other hand, if I'd known you were working yourself into a state because I wasn't here I would have thrown caution to the winds.'

'I'm not. Do you have to tower over me like this?' she asked irritably.

He laughed and sat down next to her. 'You are, you know. Why?'

She plaited her fingers and stared down at them silently, feeling defeated and foolish.

'I like your hands,' he said at last, and freed one to take it into his. 'I can't stand women with long, talon-like nails.' And he folded it into a fist and raised it to his lips. 'As a matter of fact, there's so much I like about you, Verity, that it's hard to know where to start.'

'Don't,' she said huskily.

'Don't what?'

'Flatter me...shower me with compliments,' she said drily.

'I wouldn't dream of telling you anything but the truth.' His smiled faintly. 'I also feel we should go about this a bit differently.'

'What?'

His eyes laughed at her. 'This.' He touched her cheek then spread his fingers through her hair and leant closer. 'Mmm. Smells lovely. Clean and fresh.'

'How differently?' Verity asked with dogged determination.

'I think we should talk. Talking while you're making love is—makes it extra-special. Adds another dimension of intimacy, if you like. So far we've been unusually silent.'

And so far it's been by design, Verity thought. She said, just a little ironically, 'So you gave me to understand last night, but perhaps some people are talkers and others not. Is there a sort of set pattern of excellence for it?'

'By no means. What works for some doesn't for others, but talking is a fairly spontaneous reaction, and you, for example, are seldom lost for words in other respects.'

'Brad...'

He waited.

She bit her lip, tried again, then said, 'I can't. I mean, I wasn't trying to...to...'

'Make verbal love?'

'Well, no——'

'Come up with some more objections, then?'

She winced.

'Well, yes?'

'I... Oh, yes,' she agreed a bit exasperatedly.

'Then I definitely did stay away for too long. Are you hungry?'

'No—I mean, I hadn't thought about it yet.'

'Ah. I really thought you had dinner first in mind, and I was going to suggest, seeing as you look so fresh and tidy and quite stunning, that I take you out for it—I happen to know where the rest of the mob are eating, so we could avoid it like the plague—but on second thoughts you could be right; I think we should stay here and forget about food, and that way I could reassure you and——'

'Take me to dinner,' she said with a sort of gloomy decision. 'That way I might...I don't know.' She grimaced.

'Delay the evil moment?' he suggested with perfectly wicked gravity.

Verity laid her head back with a sigh. 'If you must know, yes. What does that make me?' She turned her head to stare into his eyes.

'A fighter, my dear,' he said after a long moment. 'And a gallant one at that.'

They ate at Oskar's, which was part of the Club Tropical complex and fashioned as a grotto with rocks and pools and wooden bridges over them. They arrived to find it was their curry night, and discovered that they both loved curry, of which there were at least six varieties.

'I make quite a good curry, although I say it myself, as shouldn't!' Verity smiled ruefully and sipped the wonderfully smooth, clean wine he'd chosen.

'So do I—what a coincidence. We could swap recipes.'

'So cooking is another of your skills?' she asked as she took a forkful of cucumber and cream. 'If that's so, you and my mother should swap recipes. She's a genius, and all I know I've learnt from her.'

'I don't like conventional cooking,' he replied, looking amused. 'I'm useless when it comes to boiling eggs. But there are times when it's tiresome to be a bachelor and totally dependent on other people's cooking.'

'What about things like breakfast, though? I mean, if you can't boil eggs?'

'I make a mean omelette—perhaps it's because I don't *like* boiled eggs that I have such difficulty with them.'

'Well, what kind of things do you like to cook?'

'Oh,' he sat back, 'filet mignon, spare ribs, pan-fried fresh barramundi, barbecued lobster tails, garlic prawns—I once did some trout I caught in New Zealand in Benedictine and tinned peaches...that was all there was, and it was delicious.'

Verity had to laugh. 'I might have known.'

He raised an eyebrow at her.

'That it would be exotic and...expensive.'

He looked injured. 'Is that a slur?'

'No. But, as you yourself remarked once, your imagination is so wide-ranging—or words to that effect. Not many people would think of using Benedictine and peaches even if there wasn't anything else to hand. How come there wasn't?'

'It was at the end of the trip and I was running out of resources—I know what you're going to say, my resources were pretty exotic, but in fact I was given the Benedictine.'

'Ah. That explains it all perfectly,' she murmured.

'What kind of a cook are you?' he queried.

'I'm very good at boiling eggs, mashing potatoes, making gravy—all those uninspired kind of things.'

'It seems to me we would complement each other perfectly, then,' he said idly. 'But then, it shouldn't come as a surprise, should it? We've been doing that for two years when you think about it.'

'You mean,' she said wryly, 'all the brilliance has been on your side and on mine there's been the down-to-earth plain common sense.'

'Don't knock it. I'd have been lost without it. But I seem to remember it was not I who came up with the touch that took, will take, hopefully, the Kneg ads out of the realm of the ordinary. A touch of genius.'

'A fluke. And not terribly original, don't forget.'

'There's another side of you that's—breathtakingly inspired, Verity,' he said quietly and, when she blushed, added, 'Don't clam up on me now, or lose your appetite.'

'Well,' she said with an effort, 'tell me how you got into writing school textbooks, then.'

'By accident. I ran into Sonia Mallory at a party and somehow or other got on to one of my hobby-horses—how kids can do geography at school, for example, for years these days and never know what the capitals of most of the world are, or where the Rocky Mountains are, et cetera. So she challenged me to do a set of basic handbooks and, God knows how, managed to sell them to the Department of Education as library material. They—caught on rather well, that's all.'

Verity pushed her plate away. 'It's always fascinated me, this rapport you have with kids.'

'I hope you're not going to accuse me of being a kid at heart myself,' he said wryly.

Verity looked across at him and their gazes caught and held. 'No,' she said after a moment with her skin prickling, and lowered her lashes.

He put a hand over hers as it lay loosely on the table. 'Dessert? Or coffee?'

But she couldn't answer because her heart was suddenly pounding and she felt weak with an onslaught of desire and something else, something new and even more frightening than the physical aspect of what he could do to her just by sitting across a table from her. A flood of tenderness for him and all the facets of his personality... No, she thought, oh, no...

'Verity?'

'I think—I think I'd like to get out of here if you don't mind,' she managed to say shakily.

He did it with extraordinary ease.

And he held her hand all the way across the water gardens, stopping once as she stumbled and steadying her, taking her key from her, as she didn't seem to be able to fit it into the lock, steadying her again once they were inside.

'What is it?' he said with a frown as she stood trembling, her hand still in his.

'Nothing,' she breathed. 'Nothing—I'll be fine in a moment.'

'You look as if you've seen a ghost,' he murmured and drew her into his arms.

She hid her face in his shoulder for a moment as she fought for composure. 'No. Brad—I don't want to do this.'

He didn't reply immediately and she looked up at last, to see not contempt, as she'd steeled herself for, but that reticence and reserve she'd noticed once before, an austere setting of the lines and angles of his face that was unreadable but riveting, and her lips parted involuntarily.

And he said in a voice she barely recognised, 'Tell me why.'

'I . . . can't,' she whispered.

'All right. Don't look like that, it's not the end of the world.' But he didn't smile, and he touched his lips briefly to her forehead then released her completely. 'Will you be all right?'

No, something inside her cried. I might never be all right again—am I being a fool, and a coward, to deny all hope?

She closed her eyes and her lips moved; then she lifted her lashes and said starkly, 'No, I don't think so; please . . . stay.'

'I can't. Not platonically——'

'I've changed my mind. Sorry, you must think I'm an awful fool——'

'Verity,' he said roughly, 'it has nothing to do with anything like that.'

She tried to smile. 'It feels like it to me, if not worse.'

He stared down at her, at the sheen of tears in her eyes and the way her arms had crept around her as if to protect herself, and for a moment it was as if he debated something silently. And she found herself holding her breath.

'There would be only one kind of foolishness to my mind,' he said at last. 'That would be to regret it if I do stay, and to hate yourself tomorrow.'

'I...' She licked her lips. 'I can't guarantee that I won't regret it,' she said huskily. 'But I promise you I won't hate myself.'

'What are you doing?' she said unsteadily some time later.

He lifted his head briefly. 'Tantalising myself almost unbearably. Don't you like it?'

'I...' She stopped and bit her lip and turned her head sideways, but that was a mistake because she was leaning against a wall next to the bed and she could see at an angle into the bathroom, and see reflected in the wide mirror, a silvery image—they'd turned all but one soft light off—of exactly what he was doing. He'd taken her blouse and bra off and he was standing with his legs wide apart so that he could kiss her breasts while she had her hands on his shoulders—silly question, she thought and averted her eyes and laid her head back against the wall.

'Go on; you were going to say?' he prompted.

She lifted her hands and touched his hair. 'You're tantalising me almost unbearably too.'

She felt him laugh against her skin. 'Is that a subtle hint—in other words, get on with it?'

'No.' She ran her fingers through the springy brown curls and shivered with pleasure as he bit one nipple gently. 'Well, I would like to be able to return the tantalisation, but you have me pinned here, semi-clothed, and——'

He stood up straight. 'I love the thought of that, but first I think I should unclothe you completely.'

And he undid the buckle of her belt and unzipped her trousers.

'I could do that,' she murmured, but made no move to. In fact, she put her arms around his neck as he slid his hands beneath her briefs and caressed her hips, and raised her mouth to be kissed.

It was quite some minutes later before he got rid of her last items of clothing and carried her to the bed that had been obligingly turned down for the night. She lay with her hand under her cheek and unashamedly watched him get rid of his clothes, then she rolled on to her back and stared upwards at the draperies, and had to smile.

'What,' he eased himself down beside her and propped his head on his hand, 'is amusing you?'

'I'm thinking that the Bali Suite has fulfilled all Len's expectations,' she said softly and moved luxuriously as he put his hand on her thigh. 'I'm thinking a lot of things; that I was a nervous wreck only a short time ago and now I'm . . . like this.' She turned on her side and played her fingers down his upper arm. 'I'm thinking that you have to take a lot of credit for defusing me tonight. Thank you.' Her hand moved rhythmically.

'Shall I tell you what I'm thinking? That I regret having any part in making you feel a nervous wreck, but one reason things have been defused is that we do this so well together. It . . . speaks for itself. There is another factor at work, only I can't quite put my finger on it except to say that you seem to have changed and not just because of this.' He took his hand away from her thigh.

She breathed unevenly. 'Perhaps it's because I decided to take your advice. About talking at times like these.'

She saw his eyes narrow and tried desperately to stay still because of course, while it hadn't been an untruth, it had only been a small part of it. The truth was that she'd decided not to abandon all hope, and it had come upon her, this decision, when he hadn't tried to persuade her to do anything against her will. It had come like a curling of optimism against all odds, but more—a feeling of courage and a feeling that to be any other way would be a denial of her innermost self, whatever the outcome. A feeling that she could no longer run away from this or absolve herself from any responsibility, or, for that matter, lie in his arms and love it, then cite Primrose Carpenter as her own sort of devil's advocate or, similarly, everything she'd suffered.

For better or worse, she thought, and trembled suddenly.

'On this occasion,' he said at last and barely audibly, 'I seem to be the one without words. Why is that, I wonder?'

'It's my turn, that's all,' she responded and didn't know where the words were coming from but was dimly grateful that some vocal part of her mind and soul was supporting her. 'You said earlier that I was seldom lost for words in other respects. I guess it had to come to the fore finally.'

He smiled faintly and cupped her cheek. 'I hesitate to think what might be unleashed—no, don't take offence, I love it. I'm all yours,' he added.

She lifted her hand and laid her palm on his cheek. 'There's only one problem—my next words are about to be rather banal. I would love to be held very close right now.'

'In a moment,' he murmured. 'I would love to just look at you—am I allowed requests?'

'Yes.' Her lips curved.

He did just that. 'They are all over you,' he murmured at last. 'A lovely bloom.'

'I feel like a grape. I used to hate them. They made me feel very plain.'

'Plain.' He grimaced. 'With a figure like this? After a child, too.'

'You're—put together quite well, you know.'

'Thank you,' he replied with mock solemnity and put his hand on her hip.

'I used to,' she made a wry little gesture, 'think that women felt maternal about you. I was probably about as wrong as one can be.'

His eyes were amused. 'Did you ever feel that way?'

'No... About this talking,' she said with an effort as he moved his hand over the curve of her waist and up beneath her arm to her armpit, 'how long does it have to go on for?'

'Oh, ages,' he said softly and with a wicked little grin. 'Besides, I wouldn't dream of proceeding to the next stage without your consent.'

'You're a—something of a tease, Mr Morris,' she accused. 'I can see I'll have to deal with you— severely.' But all she did was move into his arms with a little sigh of pleasure and a murmured, 'If that's not consent, I don't know what is.'

He said into her hair, 'I might have died if we'd talked any longer.' And wrapped her tightly to him as he began the act that united them in such rapture.

They slept for a while afterwards then made love again, but instead of feeling exhausted Verity got up and ran the bath.

'What are you doing?' he said from the doorway as she lay back in its triangular depths amid drifts of fragrant bubbles.

'Just felt like it.' She glinted a smile at him and watched him run his hand through his hair and finger his jaw. 'Why don't you join me? It's big enough for two and you look as if you could do with it.'

He grimaced. But a few minutes later, lying back against her with her legs and arms around him as she soaped his chest, he said, 'This wasn't such a bad idea, after all. Are you always this full of *joie de vivre* after sex—once you really let yourself go?'

Her hands stilled for a second, then she went on soaping. 'No.'

'That was badly put,' he said quietly. 'One of those stupid things you say without thinking——'

'It doesn't matter. I could have done the same. Shall I wash your hair?'

'I'm yours to command. Hell,' he said as she squeezed a flannel over his head. 'You sure you're not feeling maternal, Verity?'

'Far from it. Brad!' she protested as he flipped over and wrested the soap from her. 'I hadn't finished.'

'What's sauce for the goose is sauce for the gander,' he remarked, wiping rivulets of water from his eyes. 'Besides, I was afraid you were going to start on my ears.'

'I told you——'

'Whatever, it's my turn to wash you. Mmm,' he lathered her breasts, 'feels good. Like it?'

But she was laughing helplessly.

'You're not supposed to do that!'

'I love it!'

'No more than I.' And he stopped washing and gathered her in his arms and kissed her.

They got out finally and once again he took her wet, satiny body in his arms. 'All my fantasies come true,' he murmured, looking down at her wryly.

She kissed his shoulder. 'And mine,' she confessed, and the laughter and fun subsided as they stared into each other's eyes.

Until he said, 'It's my turn now.'

'What for?' she whispered.

'This.' He let her go, but only to wrap her in a towel. 'Dry yourself and I will do the same, then we can don these robes so thoughtfully provided by Club Tropical.' He handed her the white seersucker robe trimmed with pink and shrugged into an identical one, then picked her up and took her back to bed, pulling the pillows up behind her.

'Stay there. I'll be right back,' which he was after popping a cork, with two glasses of champagne from the bar fridge. 'Cheers.'

'Cheers,' she repeated. 'I'm only surprised it's not vodka and lime.'

'That's good as a pick-me-up. Champagne has other uses.'

'Intoxicating ones.'

'Not in small proportions. My father always used to maintain that a good, cleansing glass of champagne before bed worked wonders.'

'What for?' she queried.

He laughed. 'I'm not too sure, to be honest.'

'Perhaps he was a romantic?' she suggested. 'Sipping champagne together at two o'clock in the morning, in bed is—quite lovely,' she said wryly and raised her glass. 'Here's to your father!'

He echoed the toast solemnly but added, 'Doing anything with you in bed at two o'clock in the morning is rather lovely. Finished?'

She nodded and he removed the glasses. 'Sleepy?' he queried.

'Mmm . . . Are you?'

He didn't answer but arranged her with her back to him, an arm around her and one hand stroking her hair. And she fell asleep without knowing it or knowing that it took him quite a bit longer to do the same.

But something alerted her the next morning to a change in him—or perhaps it was the memory of the way he'd lulled her to sleep that made her wonder if she'd given away more than she'd intended in her lovemaking and the way she'd been afterwards. And then she'd also woken to find him awake and watching her.

'What are you thinking?' She reached across and traced the line of his eyebrows. It was early, about six o'clock, and the daylight was still pink-tinged.

He stirred and pushed his hair out of his eyes. 'That I'm liable to get caught leaving your room in compromising circumstances.'

'I thought only I worried about things like that.'

'I'm only worrying on your behalf.'

'Well, you don't need to; I've,' she hesitated, 'changed.'

He caught her hand and kissed the palm. 'So I see. Was it anything I did or said?'

She considered and wondered what to tell him. Should she plunge in and confess that last night, when she'd been so affected in the restaurant, she'd deeply suspected it had been a rush of love that had taken hold of her heart? And that it had felt like that because she couldn't recall experiencing anything like it, not even in the heyday of her attraction to Barry Wood? Not that sensation of being so powerfully moved by someone. Or should she tell him his actions had inspired her to hope because that was also part of it—or should she take things more slowly? And how to know why he was...different?

'It seemed,' she said at length, 'rather twisted, for want of a better word to—— Well, it *was* something you said, I suppose. About denigrating it to...carry on the way I was, and I couldn't help feeling I was tarnishing myself in the process, if that makes any sense to you. Which is not to say I don't foresee all sorts of problems ahead for us still, but...' She shrugged delicately then said huskily, 'There are no regrets, Brad.'

He closed his eyes briefly then kissed her lips. 'These problems—let's talk about them——'

'No, not now,' she said softly. 'Guess what?'

'What?'

'It's raining.'

'Hell!' He lifted his head. 'It started off fine—it's not only raining, it's pouring!'

She laughed. 'For once in my life, my working life, I can't seem to care.'

He pulled her into his arms. 'That's my girl.'

CHAPTER NINE

THEIR luck with the weather ran out that day.

It was still pouring at three o'clock in the afternoon and the weather report wasn't hopeful of any change overnight. And, apart from having Maddy on her mind more than usual because she'd never been away from her this long and it looked like getting longer, Verity couldn't help being quietly happy in the calm, peaceful hours they spent together, watching a video, listening to music and, for once, not plagued by interruptions. The rest of the crew, obviously grateful for some time on their own, too, stayed away. Even Len Pearson stayed away until late afternoon, causing Verity to wonder a little ruefully if it was a diplomatic omission on his part.

And, when both Len and Bob did surface via the phone to claim Brad's attention, she decided to go for a walk.

'You'll get wet,' Brad said.

'I've got a raincoat—I love walking in the rain.'

He studied her for a moment then kissed her forehead. 'All right.'

'Is—something wrong?' she said involuntarily. Because that change she'd detected in him at the crack of dawn had stayed with him all day. A different, quieter sort of mood than she'd ever seen him in, and, despite the fact that she'd loved every minute of their time together, it puzzled her.

'No. Very right. Why do you ask?' He put a finger on the frown line between her eyes.

She opened her mouth then shrugged and smiled. 'No reason. See you soon...'

She walked for nearly an hour then went into the newsagent on the way back and bought a paper, thinking to update herself on world affairs, which seemed to have passed her by lately.

What she did update herself on when she got back to the deserted Bali Suite was only world-shattering to herself, as it turned out. A little item on the third page headed 'Peer and model cancel nuptials'. She read on with widening eyes. There was not a lot to read, just that Primrose, looking strained and tired, had announced to the Press that she had broken off her engagement and would be returning to Australia immediately.

She put the paper down very slowly then picked it up again and refolded it neatly, page one up, and Brad knocked briefly and entered, before she had time to gather her thoughts, with Len and Bob on his heels. But they didn't stay long, and as soon as they'd left Brad walked up to her, took her in his arms and said, 'I'm starved!'

'It's only—five o'clock, but we could get a snack sent up.'

'I'm not starved of food,' he said gravely.

'Oh—you mean...?'

'Mmm. Precisely. Can you think of any better way to spend a rain-soaked dusk?'

'Well—no,' she conceded, but it struck her as ironic that he should be more like his old self now, while she was...how was she? she wondered. A bit shell-shocked seemed to be the only comparison she could make.

'But you're not absolutely dancing with joy at the prospect,' he murmured, his eyes actually dancing with wicked little glints.

'You took me by surprise, that's all.'

'Ah. I think I can remedy that.' And he picked her up and took her over to a settee, where he sat down with her in his lap.

A few minutes later she said a bit breathlessly, 'I see what you mean. Can I ask you something?'

He lifted his head and closed up the front of her blouse. 'Fire away. This sounds serious.'

She ran her hand through his hair. 'No. But something seems to have put you in a very good mood.'

'Something has,' he agreed.

'What?'

'Not that I was in a bad mood by any manner of means.' He shrugged.

'No, but—contemplative.'

'Not so much that either, but—a bit awestruck, I guess,' he said with not a flicker of a smile. 'By you.'

'You were not——'

'Verity, you do a lot of things to me, but one thing I must insist on is being allowed to retain some mastery over my thought processes. I was.'

'Very well. May I be allowed the same privilege?'

'Of course!'

'Then I have to tell you, Mr Morris, that, to my mind, you lie with a great deal of charm.'

He looked comically affronted.

'But if you don't want to tell me I shall not insist,' she continued. 'Although you could tell me what changed things.'

For a moment she thought she detected something serious and different in his eyes, but it was gone before she could be sure. 'Other than the prospect of this,' he said slowly and moved his hands on her waist, 'I have just had a spot of good news.'

Verity held her breath and felt her heart contract.

But he went on without seeming to notice, 'Len has given us the frozen-food account.'

The relief she felt was stunning—and inexplicable. Did I really imagine he was going to tell me Primrose was coming home? I must have ...

'That seems to have come as a bit of a shock to you,' he said wryly. 'He told me he hasn't enjoyed himself as much since his wife died; he said he knew it sounded silly, but, whether the Knegs sold or not, he felt the money had been well spent because she would have loved the ads, although, of course, the frozen foods will have to pay their way, I'm sure— which reminds me, we're going to have to do a hell of a lot of consumer research on that one—— You still look stunned, Verity.'

She tried to compose her features. 'On the contrary, I never doubted you would get it. But congratulations!'

'Well, you deserve them as much as I do. What a team!' he marvelled.

'What a team,' she echoed. 'You did say, though, the frozen-food account was like manna from heaven because it's already a household name.'

He grinned. 'If I remember correctly, when I said that I was being particularly persuasive, or trying to be. But, unlike the Knegs—which are, of course, unique,' he said humourlessly, 'there's a lot of competition in the food business. And a lot of diversification. I mean, it's not only overworked housewives one can target but also teenagers, the elderly, et cetera, et cetera. And he is moving out of the traditional area of frozen peas and fish fingers into pizzas and that kind of thing.'

'I can see that the challenge has already started to get to you,' she remarked.

'As a matter of fact, it's not. The only challenge I have in mind at the moment is getting you back to the point of no return; well, I was almost there until you started asking questions.' And he opened her blouse again.

It was impossible not to respond to his lovemaking even while she had Primrose at the back of her mind, but during the dinner they had sent up she was quiet, and afterwards she roamed around the suite, unable to settle, beset by the sight of the paper every time she turned around, or so it seemed.

Until he said quietly, 'What is it?'

'Nothing. Well,' she made an effort, 'I've had Maddy on my mind a bit today.'

'You rang only an hour ago and she was fine,' he pointed out.

'I know, but I've never been away from her for so long before.'

'I hate to sound in any way callous, which I'm not, but I think you've done wonders for her: you've got your life going again, you've got a career that will help to provide for her—and I'm sure that the time you do spend with her is "quality time".' He grimaced. 'I hate catch-phrases like that, but there's probably something in it. And when you can't be with her you make good arrangements for her.'

Verity sat down and clasped her hands in her lap and said before she stopped to think, 'It's still hard to know what's best for her sometimes. Take the Woods, for example—I don't know what to do about them.'

'Go on,' he said.

'Well, it is a bit of a quandary. They are her grand-parents and she can never know her father. *They've* lost their son and only child and—and I don't for one minute have any financial considerations in mind when I say any of this——'

'I believe you.'

'But I just can't help trying to look at it from Maddy's point of view, in a family sense, if you know what I mean. Because lately I've thought of her growing up and wondering why she should be so es-tranged from anything to do with her father. It would probably be only natural, don't you think?'

'Yes, I do,' he replied without hesitation. 'Were they really as—cold-blooded about it all?'

Verity stared abstractedly before her for a long time. 'I probably didn't help,' she said with a sigh eventually. 'After Barry died they—well, we all said and did things that might not have been quite fair. But then, later, they obviously had her on their minds and they made some approaches, but the way they *did* it made me all the more determined to. . .' She shrugged.

'Go it alone?'

'Yes,' she said bleakly. 'I could see them trying to sort of take her over.'

'Verity, you said to Sonia that when you desper-ately needed help they were unforthcoming—what kind of help?'

She grimaced. 'I thought they might be able to stop him drinking—I couldn't. But they virtually accused me of driving him to it. When I told them that he'd confessed to me he'd started drinking at school they told me I was lying.'

He picked up her hand. 'I don't know them well at all, but it sounds to me as if you need an intermediary. I would say that the hurts on both side are so deep still that it's impossible for you to communicate with each other. What about your mother?'

'She's offered,' Verity said quietly. 'I wouldn't let her. Up until recently I've been so angry...'

'But now that you've started thinking of Maddy growing up with only half a family?'

'Yes, although, wise as she can be, she can't really be impartial. She adores Maddy, and she's given me so much support that I... I don't know.'

'They might listen to me, then.'

'They might if you were——' She broke off and bit her lip.

'If we had an arrangement?' he supplied.

'Well,' she hesitated then said bluntly, 'yes. Not that I'm suggesting for one minute...' She gestured and moved on, again hastily and unwisely, as it proved, 'I'd have to think very carefully before I made any arrangements with anyone, on Maddy's account too.'

'Oh, you would,' he drawled. 'Can I ask you something, Verity? How do *you* see what's happened to us? Is it still a no-regrets situation but not much more?'

She looked down at her hands in her lap. All she had on was the Club Tropical robe, as did he. And she lifted her shoulders eventually in a helpless little shrug.

'Or is it that you're not going to allow it to become any more because of all those problems you mentioned last night? The way you are now seems to indicate that they've resurfaced. I think we should at least define what they are. Otherwise they're going to rattle away in the cupboard like skeletons,' he said drily.

A curl of anger licked through her. 'It's funny you should say that because that's rather what they are. All right, let's define them. Last night, for example, you couldn't help wondering if I was always so full of the *joie de vivre*——'

'Verity, I apologised for that and you said you could easily have done the same.'

'I could,' she replied very quietly. 'I could have asked you how I measured up to Primrose in bed—it flashed through my mind the night before, I have to confess. So that's a problem, it has to be.'

'And if I was to tell you that it's *over* and done with between me and Primrose?'

Verity stared at him, opened her mouth then closed it foolishly.

He came over to stand in front of her and went on, 'Do you honestly believe I would embark on something like this just to make me forget Primrose—is that the kind of man you think I am?'

'Brad . . .' She swallowed. 'No. Not consciously or coherently. But there *has* to be a gap in your life, if nothing else.'

'And what,' he said slowly, 'would I have to do to make you believe otherwise?'

'I don't think there's anything you can do,' she said and brushed away a ridiculous tear. 'As you yourself said, there can be... a lot of things between a man and a woman.'

'I wonder how many times you're going to cite me in your own defence,' he said with a cutting little edge, then swore beneath his breath, drew her to her feet and led her to the bed.

'Brad,' she protested.

'I'm only surprised you haven't reverted to "Mr Morris",' he said and picked her up, deposited her on the bed and lay down beside her. 'What exactly are you trying to tell me, Verity?'

'I...' Oh, God, she thought, how to tell him—should I be the one *to* tell him?

'It seems to me,' he said deliberately, 'that you're trying to tell me you'll sleep with me while I get over Primrose but that's all. I must tell you that, while I thank you for such a self-sacrificing gesture, there is no need for it.'

Her lips parted and she trembled as he opened the cotton gown she still wore and cupped one full breast, tracing the aureola and crushed velvet tip until it flowered, then sliding his hand down her body to the triangle of curls that was a slightly darker version of her hair.

'Don't you see *anything* incongruous about allowing me to do this while you have the gravest doubts about my integrity?' he added with soft mockery. 'You, of all people?'

She caught her breath and was flooded with a sense of angry confusion. 'What are *you* saying?'

'That you're using Primrose as a shield again, Verity.' She flinched, and he felt it and went on. 'I thought we'd gone past all that; the way you were last night and this morning seemed to suggest it——'

'Brad, we're not discussing me; it's *you*...' She stopped abruptly and flinched.

'Oh, but we are,' he said with his eyes narrowing and a rapier-intent look in them. 'Discussing you, my dear. You and your intentions. You didn't seem to mind announcing to the world today that we were sleeping together, but tonight you're a nervous wreck again. I've noticed this blow-hot, blow-cold approach of yours before——'

'I'm not!' she cried. 'I said I couldn't regret sleeping with you and I meant it. That *doesn't* mean to say there's any future for us——'

'Why?'

She sat up furiously. 'I don't believe you can be this—dense,' she said intensely. 'I all but wrecked my life once, count one.' She ticked her finger. 'I have a child who means more to me than anything, count two, and I have to plan for her welfare—what *is* there ahead for us, Brad? An office affair? I'm sorry, but I couldn't do it, and if you imagine that's a ploy to force your hand in any way you're wrong!'

'I don't,' he said grimly. 'All the same, it's what I have in mind.'

'What?' she whispered incredulously. 'That we do try to work together and sleep together and become the object of tawdry gossip, further tawdry gossip?'

'No. That we start to plan our future more sensibly. Tell me something—what do you really feel for me?' he said almost casually.

'I...I...' She couldn't go on because her heart was pounding in the most extraordinary way.

He smiled but unamusedly. 'When you're not blaming Primrose for this state of affairs? Because I have to tell *you*, Verity, after having slept with you

several times now, if you don't feel a hell of a lot—
God help the man you do fall in love with—— Don't,'
he warned as her eyes flashed gold and she raised her
hand. 'I have no faith in your spurious desire to hit
me or throw things at me. It's generally only a cover-
up for your lack of honesty.'

'How,' she said in a raging undertone, 'you can
expect anyone to cherish the slightest feeling of
warmth for you after saying things like that to them
is beyond my comprehension!'

'Well, I can,' he said idly, 'because, while I understand why you suffer from such chaotic emotions, I
object to being your whipping-boy on account of
them, and it's often the only way to get through to
you—by saying things like that. I am not,' he paused,
'objecting to the way you make love to me at all.'

'Oh!' She lay back and ground her teeth, but that
was a mistake too because he rolled on to her before
she had a chance to escape.

'Let's approach this differently,' he said quietly. 'We
might not have realised it, but we've got to know each
other pretty well, Verity. Haven't we?'

She stared up into the grey depths of his eyes but
they were entirely enigmatic and he rested his head
on his hand and ran the other one through her hair.

'Yes,' she said ungraciously. 'Well enough to know
that you're impossible, anyway.'

'There are times when I have to return the compliment,' he murmured. 'But—are you trying to tell
me you seriously believe I would want to make you
the object of tawdry gossip or that I'd want to harm
you or, through you, Maddy's future? From what you
know of me?'

She closed her eyes.

'Verity?'

Her lips moved but no sound came because all of a sudden she was burdened with a new understanding and it came in the form of having to agree with what he said—she did know him well enough to know it. But that in itself had other consequences and she suddenly knew exactly why he had been different this morning: because she had given more away than she'd meant to—did she know him well enough to know he would take full responsibility for that? She thought she probably did, and it was something she couldn't allow to happen.

Her lashes lifted at last and they stared at each other for a long, wordless moment.

Then he said, 'What would you say if I asked you to marry me, Verity?'

She licked her lips. 'I *couldn't* accept . . .'

He smiled briefly. 'I know you couldn't, but why are you contemplating making the other mistake you admitted you made once before? Trying to walk away from it as if it doesn't exist, in other words? Why not give me a chance, at least, to prove myself? I might just surprise you rotten.'

She took a breath then sighed.

'There's a saying, you know,' he went on. 'Live and let live. I think that's what you should do. Put away your images of yourself as a confused teenager and everything that went with it. Admit to yourself that the effect we have on each other is not only electrifying but also deeply moving, and nothing that's gone before changes that—and it moves you to want me in your own magnificent way. And let us take things from there. You said yourself that any other way would be tarnishing it. And, if you could bring yourself to trust me a bit in the process, that might help too.'

'Brad,' her lips quivered and there were ridiculous tears in her eyes again, 'you could sell ice to the Eskimos. You're also a dangerous lover——'

'*Dangerous*?' He raised a quizzical eyebrow at her.

'Yes, dangerous,' she repeated firmly, 'in that you're so hard to resist——'

'Ah, well, I don't take exception to that——'

'I'm sure you don't,' she said with a tinge of tartness. Then she sighed and slid her hands round his neck. 'It's still not that simple...' She hesitated, and the phone rang.

He swore softly, then said, 'I don't *believe* this—ignore it!'

'No,' she said with an effort. 'Brad, please——'

'Well, I'll answer it!' He got up and strode over to it impatiently, but after a couple of terse interrogations he stilled, listened for a moment, then said, 'Yes, she's here, Mrs Chalmers. I—hope it's not serious?'

Verity flew up. 'What? Who?' she whispered.

'Don't panic,' he said quietly. 'It's not that serious.' And handed her the phone.

It was not, according to Lucy. Maddy had fallen off a stool about ten minutes after Verity had rung and broken her arm, a clean, simple fracture, Lucy said, that would heal with no complications; it had been X-rayed and treated, and she had a cast on and was a little bewildered by all the fuss, and, according to the doctor, broken bones weren't nearly as traumatic for little children as adults...

'I'm coming home, tonight if possible,' Verity said abruptly into the phone.

'Darling——'

'Look, Mum, I'll ring you back in a few minutes when I've made the bookings. Can I speak to her?'

She put the phone down a few minutes later with tears in her eyes. 'She's being so darned brave.'

'Braver than her mum,' Brad said softly, and traced one tear down her cheek.

Verity turned away. 'I must——'

'I'll do it. Sit down. And cry a bucket if you want to. Mums are allowed to.'

But the earliest booking he could get was on the first flight out of Cairns the next morning. And he rang Len and explained the situation and organised a ride into Cairns at the crack of dawn. He also said to Verity's intense look of frustration after she'd rung Lucy back, 'Don't feel guilty—if anyone should, I should. But, you know, it could have happened any time.'

'I know. But I should be there!'

'Well, you can't be unfortunately, and in the meantime you've got me.'

Verity stared up at him, her face pale, her eyes still anguished.

'For comfort and consolation,' he said very quietly, and kissed her gently.

'Thank you,' she said but distractedly.

'What does that mean?' he queried.

'I wouldn't feel right about—well ...' She paused helplessly.

'Nor was I about to rush you to bed, but, when you've calmed down, if it made you feel better, if it made you feel less lonely and helpless, it has to help her,' he murmured. 'You're surely not contemplating the wages of sin or anything like that?'

He saw it in her eyes before she could formulate any words. 'Listen,' he said firmly and took her hand, 'that's ridiculous. Neither of us went into this lightly, nor for sex alone—we're two adults who came together because of a force between us that we found we couldn't deny. You're not *still* of the opinion that I'm toying with you, are you, Verity?' he said compellingly.

No, she answered him in her mind. But I still can't help wondering how you'll feel when you find out about Primrose, and how much, for you, that force was generated by her desertion—the same old question!

'No,' she said slowly.

'And are *you* only toying with me?'

She blinked and started to colour and opened her mouth to deny it strenuously, but the quizzical little glint in his eyes stopped her and made her blush more vividly. 'You're . . .' she started to protest, but he stopped it with a light kiss on her lips.

'I know,' he agreed. 'Tell you what, in order to take your mind off Maddy, not to mention my mind off you, should we spend a little time trying to organise how we're going to cope without you for the rest of this—three-ring circus?'

'Oh—yes!' she said gratefully.

They worked for an hour, then he stretched and said, 'Ready for bed? You've got an early start tomorrow.'

'Mmm.'

'On your own?'

She thought about it briefly and in a matter of moments started to feel cold and lonely. 'No,' she said huskily.

* * *

But he fell asleep before she did, and it was her turn to stay awake and staring into the darkness with three separate sets of thoughts doing a slow, revolving procession through her mind. Maddy, Primrose Carpenter and why she should have called off her engagement— and Brad himself and all he'd said. But of course all he'd said had been said from a wrong premise in a sense, if not two wrong premises: not knowing about Primrose, and not knowing that she could see the weight of his decision not to hurt her... And for a mad instant she felt like waking him up and telling him about Primrose because it seemed a bit sneaky to have kept it to herself.

But the moment passed and she finally fell asleep with nothing resolved.

He woke her, and in the rush to get to Cairns there wasn't much opportunity for in-depth conversation, even though he made the trip with her. But just before she boarded the flight he took her in his arms and said, 'Take as much time off as you need. I'll ring you this evening. And remember——'

'I'll remember,' she broke in. 'Live and let live.'

'I'll miss you.'

'I know you will,' she said with a laugh.

'Well, that way too, probably,' he confessed, 'but in a lot of other ways.'

'I'll...have the same problem,' she said a bit shakily.

CHAPTER TEN

VERITY lowered the newspaper and stared at her mother over it. 'What did you say?'

Lucy put down her knitting and took off her glasses. 'I said the papparazzi are having a field-day in Port Douglas, aren't they?'

'And after that?'

'You're not deaf, Verity. How is that article you're reading titled? "Is this the man Primrose deserted her earl for?" Something like that. I said,' she looked at her daughter sternly, 'what are you going to do about it?'

'You amaze me sometimes, Mum.' Verity threw away the paper and went to stand at the window. 'What on earth do you imagine I can do?'

It was three days since she'd returned from Port Douglas, and it was only a day since Primrose had flown into Brisbane and announced on her arrival when besieged by the Press that she'd made a terrible mistake, the man she loved was right here in Australia and she could only hope and pray he'd have her back. She'd refused to divulge his name, but in a week that had been remarkably devoid of news this had only added fuel to the flame. And Verity hadn't heard from Brad since yesterday morning.

'Anyway,' she swung round, '*why* should I do anything?'

'Because you're in love with the man yourself and——'

'How do you know that?'

Her mother merely looked at her.

Verity hugged herself and made an exasperated sound. Then she said, 'Assuming that is the case, he's now in the position of having two women in love with him. Lucky him! But, if you think for one minute that I'm joining a queue, think again.'

'My dear, I can understand that you feel confused and desperate, but there's no need to be cynical and bitter.'

'Yes, there is! I *told* him he was only on the rebound——'

'He might not have been. I have it on good authority that he was impossible when things weren't going well between you, and she hasn't spoken for *him*, only herself.'

'She might as well have—what do you mean?'

'Well, how *could* she speak for him? She'd only just set foot back in——'

'No, Mum,' Verity broke in angrily. 'Whose good authority?'

'Ah. Well, if you really want to know, it was your Mr Pearson.'

Verity stared at her incredulously. 'How?'

'He rang me while you were flying home. To find out how Maddy was and to ask if there was anything he could do. We had quite a chat—I must say, I thought he was absolutely charming. And naturally when he let slip that things had been resolved so happily between you and Brad I...pricked up my ears. I mean to say, it wasn't as if I was going to get any information from you, was it?'

Verity grimaced and sighed. 'Sorry.' She sat down again. 'It's not that easy to talk about. For me, that is,' she amended, and added bleakly, 'No one else has the same reservations, apparently.'

'What are you going to do?' her mother said gently after a time.

'I think there's only one thing I can do.' Verity hesitated.

'Tell me, my dear. I might be able to help.'

'Verity?'

'Hello, Brad,' she said into the phone only an hour later.

'Verity—how's Maddy?'

'She's fine. Coping with the cast really well.'

'Good—Verity, have you seen the newspapers?'

'Yes. Yes. And you don't have to explain, Brad. I understand.'

He swore. 'What do you understand?'

She paused then took the plunge. 'That you might have two women who think they're in love with you, Brad. Which is probably highly embarrassing but it needn't be. I'm...retiring from the lists. Primrose need never know about me, always assuming you can persuade just about *everyone* who knows us to refrain from mentioning it let alone making a field-day out of it. It's the only thing to do, and *please* don't try to get me to change my mind; I couldn't.'

'Did you say *think*?'

'Think?' she repeated bewilderedly.

'Verity,' he said roughly, 'don't play dumb with me. Primrose may be the one who *thinks* she's in love with me, but you're the one who is——'

Verity put the phone down.

'Didn't take it too well?' Lucy queried.

Verity, who was actually shaking with anger, said through her teeth, 'He's wrong. And anyone who falls in love with him needs her head read!'

'He's a man with a problem, don't forget.'

'I don't know why you always side with him!' Verity cried. 'He has never told *me* he's in love with me, yet he thinks he can tell me categorically that I'm in love with *him*.'

Lucy shook her head. 'Despite the fact he's right, I would object to that too.'

'Well, I'll tell you what I object to!' Verity put her hands on her hips and glared at her mother. 'I object—— This has all the makings of a comic farce! And anyone who dares raise the subject to me again can expect to——'

'Get her head bitten off. Why don't you take Maddy for a walk? It might help you to cool down.'

'I will,' Verity said tautly. 'But listen, Mum, don't you dare have any interesting little conversations with *anyone* while I'm gone.'

'I wouldn't dream of it,' Lucy said innocently.

'You did agree with me this was the way to go!'

'I agreed that until he sorts out Miss Carpenter he couldn't expect to simply take up where he left off with you. I agreed that you should tell him you all need a bit of breathing-space—which wasn't quite what you told him.'

Verity said something incomprehensible and turned abruptly on her heel. She didn't see her mother sigh and follow her retreating form with anxious eyes.

She went into the office the next morning because she knew she had to and the longer she delayed it the worse it would be, apart from the fact that she was desperately trying to avoid Brad. And sat in front of William Morris to tender her resignation.

For a man who could often look perplexed, he looked even more so. But he also made a surprising suggestion. 'Why not take a month's leave on full pay instead, Mrs Wood? And if, at the end of it, you're still of the same mind, well—fair enough.'

Verity stared at him. 'That's a . . . very generous offer . . . no, I couldn't accept, but thank you for making it.'

'It's not that generous,' he said ruefully. 'It occurred to me you might be able to take a holiday, I mean a real holiday, away from here while . . . things get sorted out.'

Verity flinched visibly. Then she said quietly and honestly, 'Whichever way things—get sorted out, I can't work for Brad any longer.'

William formed a steeple of his fingers and cleared his throat. 'That's what Brad said you would say. He—er—rang me last night and told me that on no account was I to allow you to resign. What he neglected to tell me was how to stop you. But he's actually due here shortly——'

Verity couldn't prevent herself from glancing over her shoulder.

'They finally managed to get the last Kneg ad made, in the rain,' he smiled briefly, 'so . . . Would you at least consider speaking to him yourself?'

'No. No . . .' she said, rising awkwardly. 'Please, I'll just collect my things.'

'If I know Brad, if there's any . . . that is to say . . . unfinished business between you, it won't matter where you are, Mrs Wood, he'll find you.'

'But at least on my home ground——' Verity stopped and bit her lip, then stiffened her spine, 'I'm going, Mr Morris. I'm sorry it has to be this way; I've really enjoyed working for the agency——'

'Is that why you're running away again, Verity?'

She swung round and William Morris rose. It was Brad, leaning against the door-frame, and it was not hard to tell from the lines of his face or the glint in his eye that he was in a dangerous mood. He also looked tired, as if he might have slept in his clothes, and he hadn't shaved.

William said, his uneasy tone contrasting oddly with his words, 'Great to see you, little brother! And, of course, marvellous news about the other Pearson account—I'll leave you two alone, make full use of my office! A cup of tea, a cup of coffee!' He gestured broadly. 'Please help yourself, Mrs Wood.' And left.

'So,' Brad said as Verity stirred, 'what's it to be, Mrs Wood—I'm moved to venture that famous remark—"coffee, tea or me?" Quite inappropriate, I'm sure, but it just sprang to mind—you haven't attempted to slap my face or throw anything at me,' he marvelled. 'You're slipping up, Verity.'

'Brad,' she swallowed and licked her lips, 'I——'

'Then again, you are wearing almost the same outfit you wore the day you all but allowed me to have my way with you on the floor, just next door, as a matter of fact. Does it have any significance, I wonder?' His eyes mocked her.

Verity looked down at her white jacket and black skirt, the same black skirt, it was true, and felt the heat rising to her face. 'No,' she said shortly, however. 'It only means that my wardrobe is not that extensive. But can I ask you something? Does it have absolutely *no* significance for you, Brad, that Primrose has declared to the world that she loves you?'

'Well, I do feel she might have consulted me before making sweeping statements of that nature and subjecting me to intense hounding by members of the media,' he drawled. 'But, so far as the accuracy of what she said goes, she got two things wrong. No amount of hoping and praying will influence me into taking her back, and I'm not the man she loves anyway.'

Verity blinked. 'There's someone else?' she whispered, feeling her heart starting to pound.

'No, I'm the man who could probably make her feel better about things—or could have, that's all. She just hasn't made that distinction yet.'

'Have you seen her?'

'Not yet. The first person I wanted to see was you.'

Verity turned away with an inward sigh.

'What does that mean?' he queried.

'It means,' she said after an age, 'that I still believe you have two women who think they're in love with you and, whatever you say, I will never be able to *know* whether you feel you have to take responsibility for the way I feel, or to know whether your pride won't allow you to take Primrose back, so...' She shrugged.

'So in typical Verity style you're determined to believe the worst?'

'Yes,' she retorted, stung, and swung round. 'I honestly don't believe you know your own mind on the subject, Brad. I never have, so this, what's happened, is hardly calculated to make me feel better, and that you should imagine it would makes it even worse——'

'I never for one minute imagined it would,' he countered coldly. 'I merely hoped it would not induce you to scuttle into the nearest hole to hide. It's over between me and Primrose, Verity,' he said deliberately. 'It was over before I kissed you for the very first time and you responded so—freely.'

'So you say!' she flashed at him. 'It didn't stop you from expounding quite bitterly on Primrose's shortcomings—why would you have given a damn whom she married if it was so *over*?'

'Because, although,' he said precisely, 'there was no more romantic attachment, I happen to be fond of Primrose; I've known her since she was a kid and I thought she was making a mistake—I was right.'

'Well, you were wrong about the romantic attachment from her point of view—you're not always right, in other words, Brad. You misjudged Primrose—it's quite possible you're misjudging me——'

'I doubt it, dear Verity,' he straightened and strolled into the centre of the room, 'because you are exhibiting all the classic symptoms of a deeply jealous female, for one thing——'

'Brad—I was the one who made the bookings for you and Primrose, I was the one who sent the flowers and the cockatoo, and the bicycle *made* for two! I was the one who said to my mother that in my estimation it was only a matter of time before you married her— and then this. No normal person could fail to have doubts and you may insult me all you like—which I find strange, to say the least—but I just can't help it!'

He stood right in front of her and stared down into her eyes. 'And what difference would it make if I was to tell you that what—flows between you and me makes anything I felt for Primrose pale in comparison? Yes, all right,' he said drily, 'there was a time when I thought I would marry her too, but I kept putting it off, we both kept putting it off. Why do you think she got seduced by visions of being a countess? Why do you think I let her go? Oh,' he grimaced, 'I actually did everything in my power to stop her, everything bar the *one* thing that might have done it. But I just couldn't take that last step.

'As for insulting you,' he continued quietly while she could only stare up at him, 'my insults are prompted by your failure to understand that not a damn thing stands between us, Verity, and your persistent belief that you know my mind better than I do.'

She drew a shaky breath but managed to say quite evenly, 'Do you honestly believe anyone else in my situation would not have reservations, Brad? I don't think you're being very fair——'

'I'll tell you what I think,' he said with sudden menacing softness, 'I think that, if there was no Primrose, you'd manufacture some other escape clause. Because you're still afraid to love and trust. And *I'm* suddenly afraid of such rigidity of mind because it indicates the kind of deep-seated stubbornness that takes pride in itself; it could even be called bigotry. Well,' he shoved his hands into his pockets and smiled faintly at her, 'I tried. I don't think anyone could say I didn't try. But that's the last overture I'll make, Verity. If you should ever change your mind, you'll have to come to me.'

She said through stiff lips, 'Don't hold your breath, Brad.'

He laughed, bent his head and kissed her lightly on the mouth, 'Remember me when you're lonely and sad.'

'Your Mr Pearson rang, Verity.'

'He's not my Mr Pearson, Mum.'

'All the same, he called and was most insistent that I should get you to call him back.'

Verity sighed. It was a week since she'd stormed out of the Morris Advertising Agency, a week during which she'd been unable to settle to anything—even the urgent matter of finding herself another job.

'Here.'

Verity turned to see her mother holding out the phone to her. 'There's nothing I want to say to him or that he could want to say to me,' she protested.

'There must be, otherwise he wouldn't be ringing you!'

'There's only one thing—he's probably going to try to get me to change my mind and go back to the agency. I'm not doing it!'

'Of course not. Here.'

Verity compressed her lips and took the phone. But when she put it down about ten minutes later she was looking somewhat dazed.

'He didn't try to persuade you to go back?' Lucy queried.

'No,' Verity said slowly. 'He agreed with me entirely, in fact. He said Brad must be off his mind to expect me to have anything to do with him while there were other women roaming around the country declaring they were madly in love with him.'

Lucy grimaced. 'He has a colourful way with words.'

'He also offered me a job. Which I accepted.' Verity sat down suddenly. 'In Port Douglas.'

'*Verity*...!' For once in her life, Lucy was astounded.

'Well, it is over a thousand miles from here. I'd prefer it to be at least two thousand, but that might take me overseas, so...' She shrugged, still looking dazed.

'What *kind* of a job?'

'To be in charge of his charter-boat operation. He said he thought I had unparalleled organisational skills as well as obvious experience in the promotional field... I said I lacked boating skills, and he told me he already had that but he needed someone to co-ordinate it all... Mum, will you come to Port Douglas with me for a while? It is a lovely little town.'

'What about—the memories?' Lucy said gently.

'There can be no better way to cope with memories than to confront them head-on, can there?'

'My dear,' Lucy walked over to her and put her arms around her, 'don't cry. Of course I'll come!'

It was about two weeks later on a Saturday, a week before they left, that Sonia Mallory arrived unannounced on the doorstep with Verity's parents-in-law.

'I've come,' she said to Verity's look of absolute shock, 'because ever since I met you with Brad it's been on my mind. But I've warned my aunt and uncle that I am doing this, as *you* should do it and so should *they*, with only one thought in mind: Maddy's well-being. The time for all else is past.'

It was Lucy who stepped forward and said resolutely to Sonia, 'We haven't met, but Verity has told me about you. I agree with you, so please come in, although I must make one stipulation: it's no good accepting Maddy without accepting Verity too.'

'I can't believe it,' Verity said much later. 'They were so... different.'

'So they should have been,' Lucy said trenchantly, then grimaced ruefully.

'Brad said...' Verity broke off and bit her lip. Then she decided to go on; it was part of her plan, after all, 'He said once that we needed an intermediary. He was right. They even accepted this move to Port Douglas with reasonable grace.'

'I'm sure they'll be beating a path to your door, though.'

'Mum—do you mind? I have no intention of allowing them to take Maddy over, but I was beginning to think——'

'So was I, darling. It's for the best. Although, if we're honest, we'll probably both mind from time to time——'

'And you were magnificent!'

Lucy drew herself up to her full five feet two. 'If you can't go in to bat for your own daughter, who can you go in to bat for? But I must say,' she subsided with a twinkle, then looked serious, 'I've got the feeling they'd changed their minds somewhat about you without my intervention.'

'I can't imagine why,' Verity said wryly. 'So, life goes on. And Port Douglas, here we come.'

'I must say, I'm getting quite excited about it,' Lucy remarked.

It was Verity's turn to do the hugging. 'I don't know how to say thanks.'

'Why should you? That's what mums are for.'

Verity pondered that remark later as she put Maddy to bed, and added a drawing of a flower to her cast. She also tried to discover her daughter's feelings about the remarkable events of the afternoon. Of course, Maddy was far too young to understand that she now had a doting set of paternal grandparents, but she didn't seem to be in any way disturbed.

She did, though, say suddenly, 'Mummy make faces on the wall like that man did? I liked him.'

It was like a knife-thrust in Verity's heart, and for one piercing moment she wondered if she hadn't made an awful mistake. But of course the crux of the matter was—well, there were two things, she realised as she tried to make shadow faces on the wall. What it would do to her if she fell deeper and deeper in love with Brad Morris, only to find he didn't feel the same, and what it would do, through her, to Maddy? And if that's bigotry, she told herself sadly, I just can't help it. I'm also a mum.

CHAPTER ELEVEN

'I AM impressed, Verity,' Len Pearson said to her four months later. They were seated in her small office behind the shop front in the Marina Mirage, and what Len was impressed about was her suggestion that they branch out into day cruises, small, leisurely, intimate cruises, to the Low Isles and similar destinations that were already served by other operators, mostly on much larger, faster boats.

'In fact, I'm impressed by everything you've done since you came to work for me! Business is up, we've established a reputation for efficiency and reliability—I think it's fair to say we've filled a spare corner of the market. Would I have been invited to participate in this tourist convention at the Sheraton Mirage otherwise? Which is why I'm here!' He beamed at her with unmistakable pride. 'You're invited to the dinner at the end of it, by the way.'

'Thank you,' she murmured. 'But Len, don't forget, we're going into the off-season now.'

'That's just why I think your suggestion is such a good one. Fewer people do come up here in the cyclone season and, although you may not realise it, it gets very hot!'

'I believe you.' She grimaced.

'Think you'll handle it?'

'Oh, I will. I'm tough. I'm a bit worried about my mother, though. It's not so easy to adapt to this kind of climate at her stage of life.'

'Oh.' He looked worried.

'But that's not your problem, Len. You've already been so good to us, finding us that house on the hill et cetera.' She moved some papers on the desk. 'I'm greatly in your debt,' she added quietly.

'I haven't done anything for you I wouldn't have done for any other employee who is worth her weight in salt, Verity,' he replied equally quietly.

'Perhaps not, but you gave me this opportunity when I really needed it.'

Len sat back. 'He didn't marry her, you know.'

She smiled briefly. 'That's not to say he won't or that he won't marry someone else.'

'Have you heard from him at all?'

'Not a word.' She smiled briefly. 'How...' she hesitated but couldn't help herself '... is the frozen-food campaign going?'

Len rolled his eyes. 'It's about to hit—I think it's *brilliant*, but an awful lot of blood, sweat and tears went into it.'

'That sounds like par for the course,' she murmured. 'So he hasn't changed much.'

'No. Some things about him won't ever change either. But, while he can be one of the most difficult, temperamental characters you're ever likely to meet, he has a caring streak in him that's quite unique. For example, he persuaded me to give you this job—he even created it.'

Verity's mouth fell open.

'Mmm,' Len agreed. 'He got hold of me and told me what I needed up here was someone like you in charge. Of course,' he said modestly, 'once I'd got around to thinking about it, I would have made the decision myself, but—there you go.'

'I don't believe it—why?' she whispered.

He shrugged. 'He didn't confide that far in me. But something else he did, incidentally—and I only know about it because I happened to be in his office at the time—was to take up the cudgels on your behalf with your parents-in-law.'

'*How*?'

'Well, he was on the phone to someone called Sonia and he was telling her they all ought to be shot for the way they'd treated you. He also said she was the one who could attempt to bring you all together but would she please refrain from mentioning to you that he'd got in touch with her. Oh, dear, I've spilt the beans, haven't I?' Len Pearson said without the slightest tinge of regret.

Verity swallowed several times, then managed to say, 'Why are you telling me all this? You've never mentioned his name—until now.'

Len looked at her piercingly for a moment. 'He's here, that's why.'

'*Where*?'

'At the Mirage——'

'He can't be——'

'He is, Verity. He's here for this tourist convention; he's getting a travel writer's award. By the way, he's likely to get an award for the Kneg ads, you know. Were they ever successful! Did you see them?'

Verity closed her eyes. 'How long is he here for? Don't tell me he's using *you* as an intermediary!'

'No, he's not. He never responds to anything I say about you. *I* just thought it would be kinder to mention it to you in case you bump into him on the street.'

'But he must know you were liable to.'

Len Pearson rose. 'I really don't know what he knows, so it would be safe to say that, from here on in, you two are on your own, Verity.'

'But,' she rose too and stared at him with agitation, frustration and apprehension warring in her eyes, 'I'd just got myself over it all!'

Len's eyes travelled down her figure in a kindly, fatherly way. 'It took some getting over by the look of it. Well, perhaps he's over it too. In which case, there's no problem, is there?'

That night, after Lucy went to bed, Verity sat on the veranda in the fragrant darkness and found her thoughts turning inexorably to Club Tropical and the Bali Suite, which were just down the road. And she had to ask herself how much she'd really got over Brad Morris, and confess that the thought of his being in Port Douglas filled her with a trembling kind of sadness as well as all sorts of unanswerable questions. Would he get in touch? Why had he come—apart from the obvious reason? What would she do if she did bump into him?

She closed her eyes and her mind drifted back over the last lonely, aching months, in which the only solution to her misery had been to batten it down, work as hard as she could, and try to make Lucy and Maddy happy. She thought she'd succeeded there, although Len had certainly helped with Lucy by introducing her to friends and befriending her himself when he was in town. In fact, Verity had thought on more than one occasion that when Brad had remarked that Len should meet her mother he might have been more right than he knew, and it had struck her as exceptionally ironic.

She went to bed finally with nothing resolved.

Two days passed and Brad neither came, nor did she bump into him—and it was the evening of the closing dinner for the convention to which Len had invited her to accompany him.

To go or not to go? she was still asking herself as she closed up and walked home through the park in the gathering dusk.

'I think you should go,' Lucy said.

'I knew you'd say that.'

'Well, if nothing else, you now tell me it was Brad who got you this job and Brad who was instrumental in getting the Woods to bury the hatchet——'

'I'm only "now telling you",' Verity said exasperatedly, 'because I've only now been made aware of it!'

'Don't split hairs, darling,' her mother said kindly. 'And do go. You'll upset the numbers otherwise, anyway.'

'He might not even be there. He might have left. I haven't seen Len today.'

'All the more reason *to* go!'

Verity made a curious sound and took herself into her bedroom, where she closed the door firmly.

She went.

In an above-the-knee dress with short sleeves and a scoop neck, in a pale vanilla silk taffeta. She also wore white gloves, shimmering pale stockings and gold shoes. And stood in the wonderful green marble and glass foyer of the Mirage feeling as if her knees were knocking. But Len was waiting for her and he came across with an outstretched hand. 'Verity—you look stunning!'

'Thank you. I haven't dressed up for ages, so it feels a little strange. Is——?' She broke off and bit her lip.

'Well, he was a moment ago—ah, there you are, Brad! I don't think I need to introduce you, do I?' he said over Verity's shoulder.

Verity turned slowly and experienced the unusual sensation of all the blood going to her head then draining to her feet. Indeed, although she felt like fainting but didn't, she then felt as if she'd been frozen into immobility, unable to think of a thing to say, let alone do. For one thing, she thought dazedly, he looked so tall and distinguished in a black dinner suit with a snowy white shirt-front, despite the fact that his brown hair was still long and a bit wild. For another, after months of trying to block it from her mind, she was suddenly plagued by the clearest image of lying in his arms and allowing him to play her body like a master musician, and she started to tremble inwardly with a mixture of desire and terror because nothing had changed, she hadn't got over Brad Morris, and she thought that it was possible she never would.

He broke the spell. 'Verity,' he murmured with a faint smile, 'how are you?'

'F-fine. Fine, thanks,' she tried to say brightly and commanded herself to take hold and stop making an awful fool of herself.

'And Maddy? And your mother?'

'They're both really well. Maddy is at a play group now——'

'She's as bright as a button, that kid,' Len said jovially and took Verity's arm. 'I believe we're due in the restaurant!'

At times during the evening Verity thought it was the longest, worst night of her life, and she couldn't believe that she'd been prepared to put herself through this torture.

Brad wasn't at their table but only one table away and clearly visible, which was at one and the same time a cause for relief and torment. Relief in case she'd been dumbstruck again, torment because it was being inexorably borne in upon her that she'd subjected herself to this for one reason alone: hope, to put it quite simply, the glimmer of hope that he was here because of her. Why? she wondered wildly. If that had been the reason he would have sought you out. If that *was* the reason, why would he be sitting only feet away being charming and amusing, as only he could, to other people?

And through it all she tried to be charming and amusing herself. She even danced with Len when the band struck up after dinner, but then, suddenly, it all became too much for her and she made her excuses quietly but quite firmly to him, and he let her slip away with a frown in his eyes but no comment.

She breathed deeply and wiped her brow with the back of her hand as she stepped out into the moonlit concourse, paused as she tried to remember where she'd parked her car—and Brad said her name from right behind her.

She froze, then turned slowly, and they just stared at each other for an age.

'Would you like to walk for a while?' he said eventually. 'The gardens are lovely—even at night.'

But perhaps he realised she was incapable of saying anything, because he took her hand and added lightly, 'We could wend our way down to the beach. Have you ever seen Four Mile Beach in the moonlight? I suppose you have.' His hand tightened about hers as he began to walk, and she stumbled, then managed to put one foot in front of the other beside him. 'Now that you're a paid-up resident of Port Douglas, the beach is probably old hat.' And he guided her down a pathway and out of the limelight.

'It took me a while to find my way around here,' he went on, then stopped and turned to look at her. 'All right now?'

'Yes,' she whispered. 'Thanks... Brad, you don't have to do this.'

He started walking again. 'I'm not doing it because I have to. But I'd like to ask you a question. Why did you come tonight, Verity?'

They were walking beside a smooth lawn that smelt damp, and there was a breeze sighing through the casuarinas. The hotel pool that lapped right up to the rooms was romantically lit, but they veered away from it towards the beach. 'I... There are two things I have to thank you for,' Verity said huskily. 'Taking up the cudgels on my behalf with the Woods, and getting me this job.'

He grimaced. 'Len, no doubt. I thought I swore him to secrecy. But how are you getting on with the Woods?'

'So far, so good. They came up here for a holiday about two months ago. Maddy now has the most expensive jungle-gym in Port Douglas, but apart from a tendency to shower her with gifts they've been pretty good.'

'How are they treating you?'

Verity considered. 'With caution at this stage.' She smiled faintly and added honestly, 'I think it will probably take years for us to lose our inward animosity towards each other, but we are all trying. One of their biggest frustrations has to be being so far away now—well, there are two. Maddy just doesn't understand yet who they are. I live in daily expectation of hearing that they're moving up here themselves. But Barry's father did say just before they left that I'd done a good job with her—"I'll give you that, Verity!"' she mimicked. 'But, I have to confess,' she went on, 'it made me feel surprisingly good.'

'And the job—— Would you like to take your shoes off?' he queried as they came to the beach path. 'There's a beach when we get there.'

Verity hesitated. 'No. I'll be fine. The job is great,' she said briefly, and stopped speaking as she concentrated on the path.

They came out to the beach and it was a breathtaking sight in the moonlight, but it crossed Verity's mind to wonder what she was doing as he led her to the bench.

'So everything in the garden is lovely,' he said barely audibly as they sat down.

'No. Not quite,' she heard herself say and felt herself start to tremble within again as they sat side by side but not touching. 'I . . .' she licked her lips '. . . well, I'm worried about my mother. She's finding the heat hard to take, and in any case, although she won't hear of any other arrangement, I feel that she should be able to live her own life. Still, I'll work that one out too.' She gestured then folded her hands in her lap.

The silence was broken only by the lapping of the moon-silvered water along the shore. Until he said, 'Then it wasn't an—overture of any kind that brought you here tonight?'

'Brad . . .' Her voice caught in her throat.

'I've often cursed myself for making that stipulation, by the way, but then again it also seemed to me that, unless I put the ball in your court, I wouldn't be able to make any headway at all. So that's what I did. It had crossed my mind that I should labour for you—how long was it that biblical bloke had to? But I'm afraid when this convention came up my will-power sort of broke up. Yet I still decided—although I was quite sure Len would let you know I was here— to wait and see.'

'I was . . . Oh,' she said on a breath and wove her fingers tightly together.

'Can I tell you more?' he queried and went on without waiting for a reply, 'You seemed to be so convinced I was on the rebound from Primrose that it hit me that I had to—take it into account. And after a period of sober reflection I perceived that, from your point of view, what happened had to have a flavour of,' he paused, 'off with the old and on with the new. And that, as you were someone who had real cause to be wary of these things anyway, I had, perhaps, been a little unfair to you. Unfortunately, at the time it all hit me with such force that I wasn't able then to take such a rational view, but *since* then—well, since then,' he said and put his hand over her clenched ones, although he didn't turn his head, 'I've been able to see that circumstances might have made it all look a little odd.'

Verity discovered she was holding her breath and at the same time was intensely aware of the feel of his hand over hers. She forced herself to breathe.

'So I then set about trying to rectify matters,' he continued quietly and evenly. 'I went to see Primrose and we had it all out. I have to tell you that, while I'll always be fond of her and care what happens to her, I was not the slightest bit affected by her in the way we'd once affected each other, or the way you affect me, but in my new and more logical mood I thought, Perhaps that means I'm a rather shallow person, not to mention a cad. But, funnily enough, once Primrose...calmed down and told me her own tale of woe, it seemed to hit her that we were destined to be friends rather than anything else. Now this all might seem rather facile and a matter of mere words to you, but she's also recently fallen in love again. This time with a millionaire grazier with his own Lear jet, and, although he's one of those strong, silent types, I've got the feeling he adores her and she'll be able to wind him round her little finger. Is any of this making any sense to you, Verity?'

Oh, God, she thought, what to say? 'Why...why did you persuade Len to give me this job? When he told me, I thought it might be so you could send me...a thousand miles away from you.'

He moved his hand on hers. 'No,' he said sombrely. 'It was so that I could keep tabs on you. I knew Len would need no encouragement to fill me in on your progress; I knew I'd be seeing an awful lot of him,' he said wryly. 'I knew he had enough respect and, indeed, affection for you to make it a worthwhile position.'

'And...' Her voice had a tendency to stick in her throat. 'And the Woods?'

He was silent for a time. Then, 'I might have been wrong but I couldn't help feeling a lot of our problems were caused by a lack of self-esteem for you that they'd added to directly.'

'No, you weren't wrong,' she conceded barely audibly. 'I told you just now how I felt after a little bit of praise from them.'

'Then can you see any more problems that I should attempt to address before I tell you that for these past months I've lived a kind of hellish half-life filled with thoughts of you—and us?'

Verity blinked several times and tried to speak, licked her lips, then managed to say, 'Yes, there is one more problem. You saw the effect you had on me. I nearly fainted, I could barely walk——'

'If you think I mind having that effect on you, I don't——'

'But it could be an awful trial——'

'Not if you were my wife. That should help to take the element of surprise out of it—and be a wonderful way to channel the rest of it where it belongs. Because, and I hope you don't intend to argue with me, Verity, there is no doubt in my mind now that I love you; I can't, even though I railed against it, help but respect and admire the strength you showed, I *need* you— and how I managed to wait this long for you is a miracle, but it seemed to me to be the *only* thing I could do to establish my credibility.'

'Oh, Brad,' she whispered, and then was lost for words.

He looked down at her. 'Do you think you could at least give me some hope that I'm on the right track?'

She tried to smile. 'If you are so sure——'

'I've never been surer of anything in my life, Verity.'

'Don't forget there are sides to me that might be hard to live with. I am stubborn, I'm——'

'Do you honestly think I'm just looking for a pretty face?' he queried. 'Yes, you're stubborn and you're a fighter and you're a thinker—and it all adds up to a total that fascinates me like no other. You're also,' his voice deepened and his eyes were very grey and steady in the moonlight, 'the only woman in the world I want to make love to.'

'Well, then,' she said shakily, 'I have to tell you you were right about one thing: I do love you, and, if your life's been hell, mine has been . . .' She shook her head and silent tears streamed down her face.

'Don't.' He took her in his arms at last. 'I think we should promise ourselves something now: all the turmoil and sorrow is over, and we should just concentrate on the joy. Promise me?' He tilted her chin and stared into her eyes.

'I'm only sorry it isn't Club Tropical,' he said as he undressed her slowly in his room. 'But we could have our honeymoon there, or part of it.'

'If you only knew how Club Tropical tormented the life out of me,' she said softly.

'Well, I have to confess, that was another reason I persuaded Len to give you this job. I thought it couldn't but help to keep me in the forefront of your mind.'

'That's diabolical!'

'Mmm,' he agreed. 'But then I was in a pretty diabolical frame of mind at times. Unfortunately, when I'm without you I tend to be that way, and don't forget I not only had to work in the same office we used to share but I also had to cope with someone else doing your job.'

She had to smile. 'It's a wonder you all survived.'

He removed her bra, stared down at her breasts, then looked up with something wryly amused in his eyes. 'One thing kept me sane—do you know what I used to dream about? Your freckles. I even got to the stage where I'd start to try and count them—I only tell you this because I'm now moved to kiss each and every one of them. But,' he sobered, 'you've lost weight, my love. I'm *sorry*,' he said intensely.

'Brad, I think I might be more to blame than you, but anyway, you made me promise something just now,' she reminded him. 'That's behind us—and I can gain weight. Just you watch me!'

'With pleasure.' But his eyes were still serious.

'What now?' she whispered and touched the lines beside his mouth with her fingertips.

'I'm a little apprehensive, that's all.'

'Of...me?'

'Of what I feel for you. Having you in my arms like this, at last, makes me feel I might never be able to let you go.'

Her lips quivered. 'Then I'll just have to be strong for both of us, won't I?'

'Are you telling me you have plans to go somewhere at this moment?'

'Not at the moment, no,' she said gravely. 'But when the time comes...'

A flicker of amusement lit his eyes at last. 'I wouldn't let you go far,' he warned.

'Well,' she pretended to consider, 'you could come with me. My mother, who has remained a fan of yours through thick and thin for reasons best known to herself, will be delighted to see you. So,' she said with a soft sigh, 'will Maddy. I'm still trying to make shadow faces on the wall that live up to yours. Brad— we should talk about that.' Her eyes were suddenly anxious.

'About Maddy?' he queried.

'Well, it can't be easy to take on ... another man's child.'

'Verity, it won't be a problem, if for no other reason than that she's *your* child. And I solemnly swear that I will never treat her differently to any of our children. Don't forget, you're also talking to someone who has an innate respect for children.'

'Oh, is that how you do it?'

He grimaced. 'I suppose so.'

'I love you,' she whispered. 'I hope it doesn't bore you—the number of times I seem to want to say that.'

'I've never been less bored in my life. I hope it won't be a problem for you, the number of times I'm liable to want to do this.' He moved his hands to cup her breasts.

'I doubt it, but I seem to remember being in this position once before.'

'This position?' He moved her away from him.

'Yes,' she agreed. 'Semi-clothed and——'

'Do you really mind?'

'Not really, but——'

'Good, because I have years and years of semi-clothed, not to mention totally unclothed plans for you, my darling Verity. So I think it would be a good idea if we got married, preferably tomorrow. What do you think?'

She told him.

But it took a few more days to organise and it turned into a surprisingly large wedding. Brad's mother came, as well as William and Gloria. So did the Woods, and gave Verity to understand she'd gone up another step in their estimation, and Len flew the original Kneg crew up for one thing as well as offering them the *Jessica* for a honeymoon cruise to Cooktown and insisting they drive back through the Daintree in one of his four-wheel-drives because he said he felt sure they hadn't been able to appreciate its wonders the last time they were there. And it was certainly his doing that Verity and Brad walked down the aisle of St Mary's-by-the-Sea as man and wife with Maddy beside them and Lucy looking on radiantly—to the strains of bagpipe music.

They looked at each other.

'Not *Hamish*,' Brad said.

It was, in full regalia, standing at the bottom of the steps in the sunlit park.

'I don't know why, but now I really feel married,' Verity said softly.

Brad turned to her and kissed her deeply. 'So do I.'

WORDFIND #4

```
A L G U Y A S D N I L M N B
D W O O I Z U I R W C F R J
V G B V P A M N J X C A W E
E Q U E E N S L A N D Z X B
N F G H J R S D F M O R T N
T G V G Y W L O O H O F N I
U N U K M O G R D F W D O U
R O Y T C D R D T K Y U I Q
E R F X X I S D V T T N S Q
V T B R S W T Y G H I U S L
R S V G J B K L L I R I A R
Q M G P U T O V B N E O P A
W R L K J U Y S T Y V N B H
D A N G E R O U S H U J M X
```

ADVENTURE LOVER
ARMSTRONG BRAD MORRIS
BOSS PASSION
DANGEROUS QUEENSLAND
HARLEQUIN WIDOW
LINDSAY VERITY WOOD

Look for A YEAR DOWN UNDER Wordfind #5
in May's Harlequin Presents #1554
SECRET ADMIRER by Susan Napier.

WF4